17/30

Young Sherlock
The Mystery of the Manor House

1

The Young Master

The young man who stepped from the first compartment of the London & North Western Railway Company's mid-morning express from Crewe when it arrived at Preston on that fine November morning was unusually tall and unusually thin. He was wearing an old travelling cape of good quality and one of those curious round, low-crowned, wide-brimmed, hard felt hats that were known as 'Billycocks', some say because they had first been worn by William Coke at the great shooting parties held on his estates at Holkham in Norfolk during the 1850s.

The young man's luggage, which consisted of several trunks and boxes, was wheeled by a porter to the luggage office to await collection by 'owd Roger', the carrier from his village who journied daily to the station as part of his normal round of collections and deliveries. The young man strode briskly out into the station yard carrying just the portmanteau that contained his items of most immediate need. He glanced briefly round the yard, at the confusion of carriages, gigs, dog-carts and cabs, on the off-chance that someone may have come to meet him.

But they hadn't. No one ever did. Not any more. They had once, long ago. Indeed, when he'd first been sent away to school, some seven or eight years before, he'd always returned to find the carriage had been sent to collect him, complete with a footman in full livery. But then the carriage had been disposed of and the footman, after a blazing row with old Squire Holmes, the young man's father, and an adamant refusal to accept employment in the gardens, had packed his bags and noisily departed, some said for London and a post with 'an aristocratic family.'

After that there had always been a gig, one of those little two-wheeled, one-horse jobs, driven by a general factotum. But within a year or two even that had stopped coming. Nothing had been said. He had supposed that he must have reached the age at which young men were expected to look after themselves. And, having got over the first shock of abandonment, he had grown quite happy with this arrangement. He had come to enjoy the feeling of independence. Furthermore, he'd come to enjoy walking the six or seven miles from the station to his home beyond the village of Pendargh. It gave him a chance to savour the pure pleasure of 'coming home'.

Coming home! This time it was especially exciting. It was the first time in almost a year, for one thing. And it was to be a longer-than-usual Christmas vacation for another. This was because of a mild outbreak of typhoid at the school. Once they were out of quarantine the boys had been allowed home and the school had been prematurely closed for disinfection.

So, here he was, young Sherlock Holmes, just turned seventeen years of age, and coming home for Christmas in the early part of November in the year 1871. It was to prove a home-coming full of the most singular occurrences.

He strode out from the station down bustling Fishergate and on into Church Street and Ribbleton Lane which, in those days, crossed the Bowling Green and, for some way, ran parallel to the seven-mile stretch of railway line that served the quarries up at Longridge, not more than a couple of miles or so from his home. Soon he was passing through the tiny village of Grimsargh and here, by the church, he took a left turn and struck out across country. He emerged onto a bridle-path that ran along the southern edge of Pendargh Wood, and a short way down climbed a stile and passed into the wood itself.

This wood he knew well. Here he had often played when he was younger. And deep inside there stood an old woodman's hut, long deserted, which he had for years used as a hide-away. He knew these woodland paths, too, like the back of his hand, and he made his way quickly and deftly along them, taking the shortest and most direct route. Soon, through the bare November trees, he could make out the shape ahead of Pendargh Manor House with its mellow red bricks and cluster of tall chimneys. Here, for generations, his ancestors had lived as squires.

He broke from the wood onto the edge of Manor House lands and stopped for a moment to gaze at the old place. It was just as he remembered it. Nothing had changed. Absolutely nothing. Even the broken window in Nanny's old room was still broken as it had been ever since his father, pigeon-shooting, had shattered it with the ill-aimed barrel of a shot-gun long ago. And the rude little boy in stone who stood at the entrance to the shrubbery was still headless, his head lying sadly between his feet, recalling a bout of single-stick during which Sherlock had, one distant summer's day, floored both his opponent and the rude little boy's statue. (The statue was, in fact, of a cherub, but some departed servant, more prudish than the Holmeses, had dubbed it 'the rude little boy' because it wasn't wearing any trousers, and the name had stuck).

Suddenly, Sherlock became aware of the figure of a woman, sitting on a garden seat on the top lawn, just in front of the house. For a second he thought it was his mother and, almost involuntarily, he began striding towards her, waving and shouting as he went: 'Hello! Hello! I'm back!'

The woman, seeing him, rose quickly from the seat and, without acknowledging him, ran pell-mell towards the nearby Coach House. Had he been close enough Sherlock would have seen that her eyes were red from weeping. He would also have seen the look of terror that had passed across her face at the sight of a stranger approaching.

One door of the Coach House stood wide open. From inside there came the sounds of hammering. But, as the woman entered, all sound ceased abruptly. And then from the open door there strolled a tall, thin, fair-haired and arrogant-looking youth who was holding a stout leather leash at which strained a ferocious Irish wolf-hound. The youth, legs astride in order better to avoid being tugged down the lawn by the dog, planted himself right in Sherlock's line of approach.

'Hey you!' he shouted imperiously. 'Get off this land! It's private property!'

Sherlock, who was still some fifty yards away from him, shouted back with equal imperiousness: 'And who the devil are you?'

'That is no concern of yours,' shouted the fair-haired youth. 'Just get off this land!'

Sherlock's anger was mounting. A new and over-zealous bailiff, no doubt! Well, one word with his father would soon put him in his place! He was about to point this out when he saw the fair-haired youth bend to release the dog.

'Well don't say I didn't warn you!' And he slipped the dog's leash. 'See him off, Rajah!' he said.

The dog bounded forward. Sherlock turned and ran. The fair-haired youth roared with laughter as Sherlock, the dog closing on him, raced back across the lawn and disappeared into the woods, the dog at his heels.

At an upstairs window of the Manor House, a curtain moved almost imperceptibly. Very slowly, it was drawn back just sufficiently to reveal the turbanned head of an Indian peering sternly down.

Sherlock ran and ran. He didn't dare look back. At one point he actually felt the dog's teeth tugging at the leg of his trousers. Mercifully, it was at this point that there came a long, high-pitched whistle from the direction of the house; obviously the fair-haired youth calling the dog back. But Sherlock took no chances. He kept running, and soon tumbled from the woods and out onto the road again. By now he was quite breathless and very dishevelled. He was also extremely angry. He was about to set off for the main gate at the front of the house when he heard the sound of a horse approaching. Looking round, he saw bouncing towards him a gig, and perched on its driving seat, like a tom-tit on a mill-stone, the round, rubicund, bespectacled figure of the last man he wanted to see at that particular moment – his Uncle Gideon.

Uncle Gideon was a solicitor. He lived alone 'above the shop', as it were, in Longridge but journied two or three times a day to Pendargh usually, it had been noted, at meal times. Sherlock had never liked the man.

'Ah!' boomed the dread voice as the gig drew level with him. 'So the prodigal has returned!' And the horse was reigned to a standstill. 'What are you doing here, boy, and in that state?'

'Some imbecile up at the house set his dog on me,' said Sherlock, with as much politeness as he could muster.

'Nosing about were you?' said the Uncle. 'You should have known better. Face facts, boy, you've no right to be there. Not any more.'

No right? Was the man mad? It was his home! 'No right?' he said aloud.

'Don't feign obtuseness with me, boy', said the Uncle sharply. 'You know full well. No right whatsoever.'

Sherlock's confusion must have been obvious.

'Well, you don't surely mean to tell me that you *don't* know? I mean your father *did* write you?'

'I've had no word from father in almost a year.'

'Why bless my soul, the boy don't know!' Uncle Gideon was plainly surprised and embarrassed. He tapped the seat beside him with the flat of his hand. 'You'd best get up, boy.' And Sherlock, handing his portmanteau up first, clambered into the gig.

'What *is* the matter, Uncle Gideon? What has happened?'

His Uncle looked at him for some time in silence, obviously uncertain how best to phrase the bad news that it had unexpectedly been left to him to break. The pause seemed, to Sherlock, like an eternity. Why doesn't he get on with it? he thought.

Finally, with a deep intake of breath, the little solicitor began in typically round-about fashion. 'Fate, boy, tempted once too often by your feckless papa, has turned a malevolent aspect upon the Holmeses . . .' And he whipped up the horse, and they set off at a trot

10

in the direction of Pendargh Village. As they went, Uncle Gideon's voice rolled on at its measured and sombre pace. Odd words of what he said rang in Sherlock's · ears like the tolling of a funeral bell. 'Debts' . . . 'Creditors' . . . 'Bankruptcy' . . . 'Fled abroad' . . . 'Bailiffs' . . . 'Everything gone' . . . 'House sold' . . . 'New people now' . . . 'No right to be there' . . . 'Not any more' . . . 'Not ever again' . . . 'Gone!' . . . 'Gone!' . . . 'Gone!'

They were approaching the village now and every so often the Uncle broke off to doff his hat and call a cheery 'Good day!' to someone he knew.

Sherlock sat staring ahead of him, seeing no one. He felt numb. Why had no one told him before? Why had there been no warning? Even his brother Mycroft, good old Mycroft, that great, brilliant, idle hulk, now in his early twenties and working in Whitehall for some Department of Government, had mentioned nothing of this in his occasional letters to the school. How could they have let him come home to find both house and parents gone?

Still the voice rolled on: 'However, *you* have been granted an angel of mercy in the bountiful shape of my own dear sister, upon whom I am about to call, and *to* whom I shall be only too pleased to deliver you. Best smarten yourself up, boy. She don't take too kindly to ragamuffins.' And he doffed his hat yet again and called 'good-day!' to yet another acquaintance at the road-side.

Aunt Rachel, to whom Sherlock was duly delivered, was not a real Aunt, though she was a Holmes by marriage, her late husband having been some sort of distant cousin of Sherlock's father. She and her husband had once run a small school in the vicinity 'for the sons of gentlefolk' and this, coupled with her tenuous connections with the squirearchy, had given her some rather high-falutin ideas.

She was a tall, thin, vinegary woman, sharp-tongued and prim. She lived in a prim house and, in addition to her prim brother, had one prim daughter. The daughter's name was Charity.

Charity was a precocious fourteen years of age. She was spoiled beyond belief by her mother and her Uncle who held her up to everyone as a shining example of *all* the virtues. She was always spotless and neat and wore freshly-starched flouncy dresses. Her carrotty hair which she wore in ringlets had never so much as a single curl out of place. Sherlock hated her.

He was perched now on a hard, high, straight-backed chair in the prim little parlour of the prim little house surrounded by this prim family who, when gathered together, always seemed to number so many more than three.

Charity, sitting in the window seat, smirked continuously at him over the top of her sewing-frame. Uncle Gideon, standing at the mantlepiece, nodded his head a good deal, and dipped continually into the biscuit barrel. Both listened with mingled respect and admiration as Aunt Rachel layed down the rules of her establishment.

'We in this household,' she began, 'are governed by three simple proverbs . . .'

Sherlock, straining to appear attentive, amused himself by silently identifying the origins of each quotation as it was mentioned.

'Namely,' his Aunt continued, 'that cleanliness is next to godliness . . .'

John Wesley. Sermon 93. But a phrase probably Hebrew in origin . . .

'. . . that manners maketh man . . .'

Fourteenth century proverb. Origin unknown.

'. . . and that punctuality is the politeness of Kings.'

Attributed to King Louis XVIII of France. Hm. Three out of three, he thought. Well done! But he quickly suppressed an urge to smile, as Aunt Rachel, staring him straight in the face, asked:

'Do you suppose that *you* will be able to live by these simple precepts?'

'Oh yes, Aunt Rachel. I'm sure I shall', said Sherlock, without thinking.

'Then there are just two more things,' his Aunt continued. 'First, I should prefer that you do not wear that shabby old cape and that vulgar billycock hat when you are walking with the family . . .' Walking with the family? He hoped he wasn't going to have to do that too often!

'Second, that no further reference be made under my roof to the unfortunate manner of your parents downfall. It has brought great shame upon the family.' That really was *too* much.

'I'm sure, Aunt Rachel, that my father never did anything shameful', said Sherlock with polite firmness. Uncle Gideon at the mantlepiece almost choked on a biscuit at the very idea of anybody answering his sister back.

'Don't try to defend him, boy!' he spluttered. 'He was *prodigal*!' And to emphasise the awfulness of prodigality he thumped the mantlepiece with a pudgy fist.

'But, Uncle Gideon, in fairness . . .'

'Sherlock,' interrupted Aunt Rachel in that sinisterly

13

quiet voice that she reserved for statements against which there was no argument. 'Sherlock, there is no denying the shame. Even I, despite my own unremitting prudence have been unable to escape some portion of it. I am not complaining, you understand. We all have our crosses to bear. Furthermore, I promised your mother I would take care of you, and I am not one for shirking my duty – no matter what the cost!' And she sniffed and wiped a self-sacrificial tear from the corner of one eye, and rang the bell for her servant.

'Now,' she then continued, 'is there anything you wish to ask me before we all go about our various duties?'

There was. Of course, there was.

'Did my parents leave no word as to when I might expect to see them again, Aunt Rachel? Or where?'

'None', said the Aunt with brutal frankness.

And Uncle Gideon, yet another biscuit poised in his hand, totted up the final sum of the old squire's iniquities: 'Feckless. Prodigal. *And* irresponsible!' he boomed. Then he popped the biscuit into his mouth and began munching it rapidly, like a rabbit.

It was just then that the door opened and Aunt Rachel's servant, Mrs Cunliffe, entered in answer to the bell. She was a comfortable, homely, handsome woman in her late thirties, fresh-cheeked, and rosy, and warm. Hers was the one genuinely friendly face in this prim little house. Sherlock had known her in happier times, for she had been in service at the Manor House during the last years that the Holmeses had owned it. When she had opened the front door to him on his arrival at the Aunt's, Sherlock had been both surprised and delighted. Dear Mrs Cunliffe!

She was now instructed to show Sherlock to his

room. However, as she bent to pick up his portmanteau, which was beside his chair, she exclaimed with some concern, 'Why, Mr Holmes, your leg's all covered in blood!'

'It's nothing, Mrs Cunliffe,' said Sherlock. 'I had a brief encounter with an Irish wolf-hound, I'm afraid.'

'And came off second-best!' chimed Gideon gleefully.

Charity, who had been silent for so long now, suddenly spoke. 'That dog *may* have had rabies, Mama.' And she smiled as if pleased by the possibility. 'And *he*', she went on, nodding towards Sherlock, 'may go *mad*!' Her eyes fairly sparkled as if her deepest wish were to live in the same house as a madman.

'Charity! Whatever puts such terrible thoughts into your head!' said Aunt Rachel. 'However, I do think that leg should be looked at. Sherlock shall go and see Doctor Sowerbutts. He's a little monkey of a man with precious little knowledge of medicine, but he should be able to apply a simple bandage.'

Gideon nodded assent. And Charity giggled.

2

The Running Patterer

Sherlock was glad to get out into the street, into the open air again, away from the stiflingly oppressive atmosphere of the little house; away from the restrictiveness; away from the smugness; away from the evident disapproval. He was as yet unable fully to assimilate all that had happened to him that day which had begun so promisingly and turned so sour. Every plan, every hope, with which he had set out that morning lay now in ruins. There was just an engulfing feeling of isolation.

The doctor's house towards which he walked stood in the centre of the village. It was a large Georgian house with a bright and sunny aspect. Beside the front door a brass plate proclaimed 'George Sowerbutts, M.D.' in letters smoothed towards illegibility by years of daily polishing. Beneath, in sharp, obviously more recently engraved letters, had been added the name 'John Whitney, M.D.'

Sherlock had known both men all his life -- Sowerbutts, the merry little old man who had been a sawbones in the Navy in the days of George IV and of the Sailor King, William IV ('Sailor Billy' as they'd called him); and his young protégé whom he had rescued years ago from the Refuge for Destitutes, brought up as his own son, sent to Medical School, and finally taken into the practice. The relationship between the old man and the young was always good-humoured, albeit argumentative. It was a relationship further cemented by the fact that John Whitney, now 26 years old, had, just that summer, married old Sowerbutts' pretty and vivacious young niece, Charlotte, and all three of them were now living together in happy companionability.

Sherlock's arrival at the house was greeted with considerable warmth and pleasure. He was swept into the large room where the doctors worked and was soon sitting in a comfortable arm-chair while Doctor Sowerbutts bandaged his leg. Charlotte poured him glasses of delicious home-made lemonade; John Whitney plied him with cake. There was a big fire blazing in the grate, and he was at last warm and relaxed and beginning to feel better able to be objective about things.

Neither John Whitney nor Charlotte made any mention of what had happened to his parents, and he knew that they were trying to spare him pain, and he was grateful. But poor old Sowerbutts, with all the innocence of the absent-minded, inadvertently brought the subject up to his own intense embarrassment, and quickly put it down again with the assurance, 'They'll bounce back. They always do.'

'Oh yes', Sherlock had replied with what he hoped would pass for conviction. 'I expect to hear from them any day now. I shall most probably join them in France.'

Oh, how he wished that were true! His mind was being constantly invaded by pictures of earlier holidays that they had spent together. He saw momentarily his mother, dressed in flowing blue silk and a wide flower-bedecked straw bonnet, her arms full of roses, laughing at him as he took his first tumble from a horse. He saw his father sitting by the river fishing, as he did sometimes for days on end, beside him several bottles of Montrachet and a hamper that was a veritable cornucopia of edible luxury. He saw the shimmering silver fish as they were pulled from the water amid triumphant yells, and he could almost smell the wood-smoke from the fire over which father and son had cooked them in the open air.

But these pictures from the happy past were already being overlayed by others more recent and more curious. The woman on the lawn, for example. And the young man with the dog. Sherlock had an intense desire to know more about these people who had usurped him and his family.

'I say, John,' he said to Doctor Whitney suddenly. 'What do you know about the new people up at the Manor House?'

'The Turnbulls?' replied the young doctor. 'Not a lot. They keep themselves pretty much to themselves, and do little entertaining. But they're very well thought of locally. And they head the subscription lists of all the charities.'

'He was a Colonel in the Indian Army,' said old George Sowerbutts, trying to tear the bandage with his teeth, prior to tying the knot. Doctor Whitney handed him a pair of surgical scissors. Sowerbutts placed them carefully on the floor beside him and carried on tugging at the strip of linen with his teeth. 'I met him once in the Tap Room of the Bull Hotel, Preston', he went on, ignoring the interruption. 'Nice feller. Crack shot. You know. Tigers.' And miming the action of a huntsman firing a rifle, he shouted 'Bang! Bang!' and everybody jumped.

'Mrs Turnbull is none too strong apparently,' said Charlotte Whitney. 'She doesn't go out much. A delicate constitution weakened by her years in India.'

'Really,' said Sherlock.

'So they say,' added John Whitney. 'I haven't attended her myself.'

Sherlock then described his arrival at the Manor House earlier that day. He described, as well as he was able, the woman he had seen sitting on the lawn. She was small, plumpish, dark-haired. A woman of forty perhaps. Middle-aged, certainly.

There was general agreement that this description fitted Mrs Turnbull. And as there were no other women at the House, as far as anyone knew, and all the servants were Indian, there seemed no reason to think it was anybody else.

'Curious,' murmured Sherlock. 'You see, as I approached her she got up and ran like the wind. Hardly the action of a woman with a weak constitution, would you say?'

'That certainly doesn't sound like our Mrs Turnbull,' said John Whitney. 'She's usually carried about the grounds in a litter.'

'A palkee, Johnny. That's the proper name for what she's carried about in,' said Sowerbutts, who was a stickler for accuracy if he thought he knew something that nobody else did. 'It's Indian. The Colonel told me.' And he looked at them all with great superiority as the only man who had been taken into the Colonel's confidence.

'And what of the young man with the dog?' asked Sherlock.

About him there were no doubts at all. 'That must have been young Jasper, the Colonel's nephew, a conceited young puppy who likes to think of himself as the Young Master,' said Doctor Sowerbutts.

Sherlock's dislike of the youth was, if anything,

intensified.

But there now occurred a diversion which even Sherlock was unable to ignore. From outside in the street there suddenly came a shout of 'Murder! Murder! Murder most foul!'

'Natty Dan!' cried Sherlock, recognising the hoarse cockney voice.

'Aye,' said old Doctor Sowerbutts. 'The annual visit.'

'I have every gory detail, death cell confession and repentance from the gallows tree,' the voice bellowed, growing closer and closer. 'One penny is all I ask! Just one penny!' He was right outside the gate now. And the shouting suddenly gave way to a hacking cough.

'He'll be wanting his usual cough cure, I don't doubt,' said Sowerbutts. 'Charlotte, open the front door, me dear. Johnny, put away the best port and get out a bottle of the medicinal.' And they all jumped to it. Natty Dan was well-known in the neighbourhood. He was well-known in a good many places. He was one of a dying breed of men they called 'running patterers'. He travelled the country selling broadsheets, and death cell confessions and, for a small sum, would recount in lurid and graphic detail the most gruesome of recent and not so recent crimes. If these crimes were insufficiently gory, Natty Dan and his ilk would 'colour them up a bit'. If you could read, you paid a penny for the broadsheets; if you couldn't you got the tale direct from Natty's own inventive lips for the same price. Such men were, of course, fast disappearing, victims of cheaper and more widely available newspapers. Natty Dan must have been one of the very last of them.

Sherlock heard the front door close. Shortly after this he saw the door of the surgery edge very slowly open. A face appeared round it. It was a worn and weather-beaten face, but sharp and perky, the eyes dancing with life. They quickly took in Doctor Sowerbutts and Doctor Whitney, and the mouth had already opened preparatory to a renewed bout of coughing, when they lighted upon Sherlock.

'Well, well, well, it's young Master Sherlock!' And the little bird-like man slid into the room.

Sherlock had known him for some years. His father had always invited Natty into the house for a hot drink and a bite of food and on many occasions they'd sat round in the kitchen and listened to the tall tales the little man had to tell. Indeed, as far as he knew, it may have been Natty Dan who had first sparked that consuming interest in crime and the criminal which was to remain with him.

'Hello, Natty. It's good to see you,' he said. And the little man's grin grew so broad that it looked as if his face might fall in half. Energetically, he began to ferret in the ragged old bundle that he always carried slung over one shoulder.

'I've got one here you'll like . . .' he said. Then it obviously occurred to him that he had quite unintentionally ceased his coughing before receiving the looked-forward-to medicine. And he began to cough violently.

'Alright! Alright!' said Doctor Sowerbutts, kindly. He'd seen the performance many, many times before, but was always generous to itinerants. 'Give him his medicine, Johnny.'

And John Whitney poured a large glass of port and handed it to the patterer. Natty Dan took it and downed it in one.

'Oh, that is powerful good medicine!' he croaked.

21

'Why, my poor parched throat feels already more supple, my vocal chords more flexible.' And he began ferretting in his bundle once more. 'I say,' he went on, 'how about this – a genuine London crime. Most horrible mutilation by an unnatural mother. She burned her baby in the copper in a house in the Harrow Road. Worth a penny, eh?' and he stuck out his hand in anticipation.

'Of anybody's money,' said Sherlock. And he began rummaging through his pockets. 'You see, John,' he said to John Whitney, 'in recent years I have applied myself to the study of the inordinate cruelty of which human beings are capable. Can we ever truly understand such things, I wonder?' By now there wasn't a pocket left unsearched. But no coin had come to light. 'Oh, I appear to be temporarily embarrassed,' he said, as if surprised. 'Have you a penny you could lend me, John?'

John Whitney, who had been watching his efforts with a wry smile, was in fact already holding a penny-piece in his right-hand trouser pocket in anticipation of the request. He now handed the coin to Natty with a good grace.

'A thousand thanks!' said the patterer. And he bowed so low that his head almost touched the carpet. Having thus secured his first coin, he was quick to press his advantage. 'And how about this?' he went on, launching into what he obviously considered to be a dramatic *pièce de résistance*. 'An entire family massacred – cut, hacked, and battered as only a madman or a savage could have effected it. In a lonely smithy, in a remote part of that county that they call Buckinghamshire.' He paused to give added effect to what was coming. 'No less than nineteen dead.' And he looked from face to face expectantly. 'It's the very latest sensation, I do assure you.'

'The Denham Massacre!' said Sherlock like a shot. 'It took place over a year ago. And the number killed was, in fact, seven.'

Natty was momentarily put off balance. 'Maybe. Maybe,' he said. 'Poetic licence, dear boy. Anyway, *I* have the full and only true account of the trial of the murderer.'

'John Jones, alias Jenkins, alias Reynolds, alias Owen,' rattled Sherlock. 'The key witness in the case was a bricklayer named Charles Coombes who said that Jones had come to his lodgings on the Saturday afternoon ''in an old corduroy suit'', but that on the Sunday he was ''in a *good* suit'' and ''flush with money, treating both girls and men.'' '

It was game, set and match to Sherlock. And Natty Dan conceded defeat.

'I'm on my way,' he said, slinging his bundle back over his shoulder. 'I go next to that haunt of happy memories, the Manor House.' And with a wicked glance at Sherlock, he added, 'I've not been there since the new owners took up residence.'

'Then I hope they afford you a better welcome than they did me,' said Sherlock bitterly.

'They will, dear boy. They will,' said Natty without knowing what sort of welcome Sherlock had had anyway. '*I'm* welcome everywhere!' With a cheeky smile he bowed his way backwards from the room like some old actor-manager taking a curtain-call. A few seconds later they heard the front door slam.

'Welcome everywhere, indeed! There's only two doors in this part of the world have ever been open to him, and that's this one and your own father's,' roared

George Sowerbutts, nodding at Sherlock.

'Plus the jail-house door in Preston, no doubt!' added John Whitney.

All three of them roared with laughter.

Natty Dan's arrival at the Manor House later that day was announced by an Indian servant named Anil, who, having received strict instructions to inform his Master of every single stranger who called at the House, told the patterer to wait at the kitchen door and straight away carried word to the occupants of the great Drawing Room.

There were, at that hour, two occupants. One of them was the arrogant, fair-haired youth who had set the dog on Sherlock, the young man they called Jasper. He was lounging on a settee cleaning a shot-gun. The other was an Indian, tall and turbanned, who stood at the sideboard preparing a tray, laying it with wine glasses and a decanter of wine.

'Excuse me, Ranjeet, sahib,' said the young Indian, 'there is a pedlar at the kitchen door. He peddles tales of murders and crimes, sahib.'

The tall Indian waved his hand impatiently. 'Then give him a penny and send him on his way,' he said.

The young Indian was about to leave the room, when Jasper, putting aside his gun, stopped him. 'No wait,' he said. 'Have you seen this man before?'

'No, sahib,' replied the servant, somewhat puzzled by the question.

'How tall is he?' asked Jasper.

'Tall, sahib?' said the servant, yet more puzzled. 'Oh, only very small.' And he held a hand somewhere about the level of his chin and hovered it about for a moment or two, up and down, trying to arrive at an

lid shut. It was then that he heard the voice. 'I play the piano ever so much better than you play the violin,' it said, and he turned to see Charity peering in at him.

'Hello, Charity,' he said, forcing a smile. And he beckoned her in. 'Here, I've something to show you.' And he put a finger to his lips, warning her to silence.

'What?' asked Charity, suspiciously.

'Here.' And as Charity approached, Sherlock took up a small wooden box that lay on the bed. Holding it in one hand, and lifting the lid with the other, he held the box out to her. Inside lay a human thumb. Charity peered at it fascinated.

'Oh! What is it?' she asked.

'That, Charity, is the thumb of Calcraft the Hangman,' said Sherlock with impressive solemnity.

'Ooooooo!' her eyes nearly popped out of her head.

'And when that thumb senses the presence of an informer or a sneak, do you know what it does?'

'No. What does it do?' asked the girl.

'It rises slowly up – and it waggles,' said Sherlock. 'Look!' And sure enough, the thumb rose slowly in the box, and waved itself about. It was, of course, a trick box, and the thumb was Sherlock's own poked through a hole in the bottom, but the trick worked a treat.

'Oh! You horrid boy!' squealed Charity. 'I shall tell Mama when she returns. You just see if I don't.' And she slammed out of the room.

Sherlock smiled triumphantly. And it was at that very moment that a handful of gravel showered against the window. He looked out to see Natty Dan standing in the garden below.

'Sherlock! I've something to tell you!' shouted the patterer.

'Ssshhh! Not so loud!' said Sherlock from above.

27

'Go round to the kitchen door. I'll be down directly.'

In the kitchen he experienced some difficulty with Mrs Cunliffe who strongly disapproved of admitting the likes of Natty and finally gave in only after Sherlock had pleaded with her and she had been given time to gather up from the kitchen table all the silverware that she had been in the process of polishing.

'Well? What do you want?' asked Sherlock as the patterer slipped into the room, and Mrs Cunliffe with a toss of her head and an apronful of silverware swept out. 'I warn you, I haven't a penny in the world to spend.'

'No, no, no. It's the new people up at the house, dear boy,' said the patterer. 'What a welcome!' He was in a state of high excitement. 'Sat down and waited on, I was. At a great shining table. By an Indian tall as a tree. Food and wine, and fruit and wine, and food and wine and fruit. Pineapple,' he said with great satisfaction.

'Pineapple?' said Sherlock, not believing a word of it.

'And huge golden oranges and apples as big as a man's head,' continued Natty.

That did it.

'Your failing, Natty, as I have always told you, is that you push credibility to the limit,' said Sherlock.

'I go back again this very night,' continued the patterer, ignoring Sherlock's slight. 'By their invitation, pressed upon me, I might add. And tomorrow I shall *bring* you a pineapple - disbeliever!'

'Very well,' agreed Sherlock. 'But you'd best not come here. We shall meet at my old hide-away in the woods. The woodman's hut, remember?'

Natty remembered well. 'And if you don't bring a

pineapple,' Sherlock went on, 'I shall expose you throughout the county for the trifler with the truth that you are!'

Suddenly, with a crash, the kitchen door was flung open. And there, like an avenging angel, stood Aunt Rachel, with Charity at her heels.

'What in Heaven's name is that man doing in my house?' said the Aunt, in an icicle voice.

Natty Dan quickly pulled a watch-chain from his waistcoat pocket. There was no watch on the end of it, but he held it in the palm of his hand for all the world as if there were, and no one was any the wiser. 'Good Lord! Is that the time!' he exclaimed. And then to the sour-faced Aunt, 'A thousand pardons, lovely lady, but alas I must depart. I am due at the Manor House to partake of pineapple.'

And with a bob of his head to Aunt Rachel and a gleeful wink at Sherlock he nipped out of the back door and was gone.

The Aunt glared thunderously at Sherlock. The storm was about to break. Behind her stood Charity, smug and smirking. She had revenged the incident of the hangman's thumb and was going to enjoy every minute of it. Sherlock could have hit her.

3

The Track of the Three-Legged Dog

When Sherlock arrived at the hut next morning to keep his appointment with Natty Dan, he was carrying on his shoulder one of his tin trunks, having decided to distribute those belongings that had been banished from Aunt Rachel's home between his hide-away and the doctor's house.

As he entered the hut he could just make out in the gloom the figure of Natty Dan sitting on the floor leaning against the end wall. 'Alright, Natty,' he said. 'Where's the pineapple?' There was no reply.

Lowering his trunk to the ground, he went across to where the patterer sat, his legs folded under him, his face and body turned to the wall. Sherlock shook him gently. Natty Dan just toppled over. As he lay there, a shaft of sunlight streamed in through a crack in the roof of the hut, and fell right across him. Sherlock could hardly believe what he now saw. The old patterer's weather-beaten face was fixed in a hideous deathly grimace as if he had, in his last moments, been witness to the most appalling horrors.

Sherlock found himself momentarily unable to move. He gazed down at the old man and couldn't even cry out. He was numbed. It was only now that Sherlock realised what Natty had meant to him. Yet another link with the past had just been severed.

He then noticed that clenched in one of Natty's fists there was a stub of white chalk. He turned again to the wall against which the patterer had been leaning.

There, just a few feet up from the floor, were scrawled in fresh chalk letters the words, 'Haybay Old Mo.'

'Haybag Old Mo,' he repeated to himself. 'What were you trying to tell me, Natty?'

Suddenly, the hide-away that had hitherto held so many happy memories for him, felt chill. And though the November sun shone quite strongly that day, the chill seemed even sharper as, later that morning, Doctors Whitney and Sowerbutts, summoned to the hut, completed their preliminary examination.

Natty Dan's body lay now covered by a sheet. But beneath the sheet Sherlock fancied he could still see that face, frozen in its deathly grin. There were no obvious signs of violence, but the doctors decided finally to remove the body to the surgery.

Sherlock was left alone with the sole local representative of the law, one Sergeant Silas Grimshaw. Grimshaw was a burly Yorkshireman, mightily convinced of his own ability, which was, in fact, extremely limited. He had come to the area only a few months previously amid much jocular speculation as to why his home county may have got shot of him. He stood now in front of Natty Dan's last message, copying it laboriously into a brand new note-book with a brand new pencil. Where notebooks and pencils were concerned, Sergeant Grimshaw was a most fastidious man.

'Haybag Old Mo,' said the policeman as he wrote.

'Haybag means woman,' said Sherlock brightly from just behind him.

'Really,' said the Sergeant with great coolness.

'It's patterer's cant. Slang, you know,' offered Sherlock.

'Is it now,' said the Sergeant.

31

'Mind, the "Old Mo" puzzles me,' said Sherlock rapidly. 'Possibly a woman *called* Old Mo, I suppose. A nickname. They all have them. Maybe he wanted me to find a woman known on the road as "Old Mo". Maybe she had something to do with his death.'

'Now hold your horses, lad,' said the Sergeant very firmly. 'We're not even sure yet how he died.'

But Sherlock's mind was racing ahead. 'How would I set about finding such a woman?' he asked.

'You want my advice?' said the policeman. 'Don't worry your head about it, lad.'

'But Natty Dan was clearly trying to tell me something,' Sherlock persisted.

'And you have now told the police,' said Sergeant Grimshaw, with great paternalism. 'Correct procedure. Very commendable. I shall mention the fact in my report.'

'Thank you,' said Sherlock, not in the least impressed by this promise.

'Now you state that the deceased was last headed *back* to the Manor House?' said the policeman, recapitulating on an earlier conversation.

'That's what he said,' said Sherlock. 'That he had been in, and been feted, and that he had been invited back.'

'Then maybe I'd best have a little word with Colonel Turnbull.'

'You know it occurs to me . . .' began Sherlock, quite keen at this stage to share any ideas with the police. But he got no further.

'Leave it, lad,' cut in the Sergeant. 'Just take my advice, get along home and don't worry your head about it.' And ducking his head to avoid knocking his helmet off on the low door-frame, he left the hut, heading back towards the Manor House.

'Pompous ass!' said Sherlock quietly to the departing back. And he kicked an old boot across the hut, by way of letting off steam.

Later that day, Doctor Whitney confirmed the cause of Natty Dan's death. 'Heart failure induced by tetanus,' was what George Sowerbutts eventually wrote on the death certificate.

'But his face? That horrible expression!' said Sherlock who, for some hours, had been perched on a chair in the surgery awaiting the outcome of their examination.

'Ah-ha, what you saw there, young'un,' said old Sowerbutts, 'was what we call the Hippocratic smile, the old *risus sardonicus*, as the ancients called it.' And he pulled his face into a mask-like grimace and held it, glowering at Sherlock, by way of illustration.

John Whitney explained. 'Extreme muscular contraction is one of the characteristics of tetanus,' he said. 'The expression is caused by a spasm of the facial muscles.'

'Muscles go hard as a board,' put in George Sowerbutts, and this time he stuck a rigidly-held arm out to illustrate his point.

'That'll do, George!' said John Whitney, disapprovingly.

'And what would be the cause?' asked Sherlock.

'May I tell him, Johnny?' said the old doctor. 'Or are you afraid that my description might offend his delicate sensibilities?' And he winked at Sherlock.

'No. You can tell him,' replied John. 'Just try not to be lurid.'

'In a word, young 'un, *dirt*,' said Sowerbutts. 'From

33

the smallest wound. Soil. Manure. Road sweepings. Even something as simple as a scratch from a rose thorn has been known to prove fatal.'

'Someone like Natty Dan would be especially vulnerable,' added John Whitney, 'by the very nature of his way of life.'

Some little time later, Charlotte Whitney showed Sergeant Grimshaw into the room. He was delighted to learn that medical opinion favoured tetanus as the cause of death. 'Natural causes!' he said with great finality. 'That's what we like. An open and shut case.' Then turning to Sherlock, he said gravely, 'And I've a little advice for you, my lad. That there Natty Dan of yours spun you a right old yarn, you know. He only went to the Manor House once, and he didn't as much as set foot over the threshold. Sent him packing right off, they did. You've got to learn to sort the wheat from the chaff, you see.' And then he added, with all the superiority he could muster, 'It comes with experience.'

'And what about Old Mo, then?' asked Sherlock, who strongly objected to being treated like a child by this complacent policeman.

'Don't worry your head about it, lad,' said Grimshaw, annoying him yet more. 'It's not your concern.' And with a 'Good-day, Mrs Whitney. Gentlemen,' he strolled from the room. Sherlock sat motionless, silent, fuming.

Just then the marble clock on the mantelpiece struck the half-hour, and glancing at it, Charlotte said, 'I say, Sherlock, have you seen the time? Shouldn't you be getting along home?' It was now half-past noon.

'Oh, don't *you* start!' said Sherlock, sharply. It seemed that everybody was now determined to treat him like a child.

'But you've been out since first thing this morning,' persisted Charlotte. 'Your Aunt Rachel will be getting worried about you.' And trying her best not to appear to be throwing him out, she led him from the room and towards the front door. Sherlock allowed himself to be led. He was deep in thought, and not listening to a word she said. By the time he reached the front door, he had already decided upon his next move.

As it happened, Aunt Rachel was not in the least worried about Sherlock's whereabouts. On any normal day, she most certainly would have been. But this day had already turned into a most abnormal one for her, just as it had for Sherlock, and the reasons, though quite different, were not unconnected.

In the parlour of the prim little house a bad-tempered Charity was standing on a low stool surrounded by a litter of dresses. There were dresses everywhere. Not a single piece of furniture but didn't have its dress draped over it in some manner. Dresses of every colour and every shape and every fabric.

One by one, for almost an hour now, these dresses had been held up in front of Charity in the hope that one of them might gain her approval. Thus far none had. So the process was continuing, though there remained very few dresses that had not already been tried and rejected.

Aunt Rachel now held up a red velvet dress trimmed with lace at the collar and cuffs and worn with a wide silk sash. 'There!' she said. 'How does that one look?'

Charity pulled a face. '*I* hate it!' she said sullenly. 'Why can't I have a *new* dress. Mama?'

'Because there isn't time, my pet,' replied her

35

mother. 'Besides some of these dresses have hardly been worn.' Charity grimaced. 'Ah!' said Aunt Rachel pointing to a dress that Mrs Cunliffe was just about to pass by. 'What's that you have there, Mrs Cunliffe?'

'Here you are, Mum,' replied the servant, handing the dress across. 'Mind it's not as pretty as some we've seen. Leastwise, not to my way of thinking.'

'How about that, dear?' asked Aunt Rachel, ignoring the menial's opinion and holding the dress up to Charity.

'Yes, that's quite pretty,' said the girl.

'It's *very* pretty!' confirmed her mother.

'But it's too short!' said Charity.

'Mrs Cunliffe will soon see to that, won't you, Mrs Cunliffe?' said her mother, passing the dress to her as if she expected her to be pretty sharp about it.

It was now that the door opened, and Gideon walked in. He looked round the room with its profusion of clothes in utter astonishment. He glanced at the table and could hardly believe his eyes. He drew his watch from his waistcoat pocket and peered at it closely and exclaimed, 'Good gracious merciful Heavens, Rachel! What *is* going on!' Then he peered at the watch again, and continued. 'Can this gold half-hunter that once graced the waistcoat pocket of our dear father, and which to my own knowledge has kept perfect time for nigh on a quarter-of-a-century, now, suddenly, be wrong! It is *not* approaching one of the clock?' And he made a great palaver of holding the watch to his ear, and shaking it, and then peering at it, and then holding it back to his ear again. And Charity giggled dutifully.

'Oh! Snakes alive!' said Mrs Cunliffe. And she ran round the room like one of Fagin's boys nicking up the dresses and, having gathered them all, rushed from the room towards her neglected duties.

'Luncheon will be a little late today, Brother Gideon,' said Rachel as the servant disappeared. 'We have had *such* a morning! I have *such* news!'

But Charity beat her to it. 'We have been invited to take tea at the Manor House tomorrow afternoon!' she announced smugly.

Gideon beamed. 'Really? Have we?' he said. And then, worried lest the invitation should apply only to the ladies, '*All* of us?'

'*All* of us!' said Aunt Rachel. 'Did I not suggest to you, Brother Gideon, that *certain* benefits might accrue as a result of a *certain* act of charity performed by *certain* people for the good of a *certain* person?' If she had meant to be mysterious, she had succeeded. Brother Gideon was completely mystified. It was only after some thought that he realised it must be Sherlock she was referring to. 'Oh *him*!' he said. 'Is he coming, too?'

'But of course, he is,' said Rachel, who always grew more charitable as advantage accrued from her acts of charity. 'You know, he's really not such a bad lad.'

Charity, who disliked the idea of her mother warming to anyone but herself, said quietly from the window seat, 'But he's going to be late for luncheon again, even though luncheon's going to be late!'

Sherlock was not merely going to be late for luncheon, he was going to be absent from luncheon. He had left the doctors more than ever convinced that something was amiss, and had decided to return without delay to the hut in the woods. By now the sunshine had gone. The sky was grey and overcast. And as he walked back under the bare November trees, he again felt chill.

As soon as he arrived at the hut, he went inside and

began a thorough search, without really knowing what he was looking for. At that time, a magnifying lens was well beyond his financial reach, but his eyes were uncommonly sharp and he examined the floor minutely in the gloom, painstakingly sifting the deep dead leaves and similar debris of past autumns through his hands. However, the only object that claimed his attention was a single and unusually large rose thorn. Being an avid collector of the unusual, he slipped it into his pocket.

Then stepping outside the hut he began a similarly thorough examination of the ground about the hut doorway. Here, he noticed the clear impressions of recent animal tracks. There were several sets, and they had obviously been made by several different animals, and at various times. However, one set struck him as curious. Not being an expert in such matters, he decided to enlist the help of someone who was, the lad known locally as Newbugs. And he set off at a trot towards the village, to find this perpetually elusive youth.

Newbugs was a lad of perhaps fifteen or sixteen years, but one of those curious children who appear to have been born old. He and his father, a man much given to violence, had arrived in the village out of the blue some five or six years previously. They lived gypsy-fashion in a tiny tumble-down cottage near the old railway that served the local stone quarry. To the villagers they had become known simply as 'Oldbugs' and 'Newbugs', and village children had been forbidden to go near them 'in case they caught something', for both the old man and the lad, it was said, were 'crawlin' with 'em'. Sherlock with his facility for strange friendships, had come to know

Newbugs through many meetings in the woods, the lad being an inveterate poacher. He was, indeed, highly proficient in all country skills and pursuits.

Some several hours after leaving the hut that day, and having searched all the possible 'hides' that Newbugs used, Sherlock finally tracked the lad to ground among the rock outcrops of an isolated fell to which he always ran when his father's violence towards him became unbearable. Their reunion was joyful. Now, happily together again, the two tall, gangling youths, strolled back towards the hut side by side, silent in companionship.

'Well, do you know what they are?' asked Sherlock when they got there, pointing to the curious set of tracks outside the hut door.

'Yes,' said Newbugs, who was sparing with words, and never volunteered information.

'What?' said Sherlock.

'You think,' said his friend. This was obviously to be a lesson.

'A fox?' tried Sherlock.

'No!' said Newbugs, with considerable scorn.

'Very well, a dog then?'

Newbugs smiled and nodded, pleased at his pupil's progress. 'Yes!' he said.

'Have you any idea what sort of dog?' asked Sherlock.

'A big dog,' replied Newbugs.

'Well, I can see that!' said Sherlock, who sometimes took exception to his friend's air of superiority. 'What kind of dog?'

'Look,' said Newbugs, and he knelt, carefully pointing out the detail of shape and pattern in the foot-marks. 'Retriever. Ordinary Labrador retriever.'

'Ah-ha!' countered Sherlock, pleased to be able to prove him wrong. 'Not an *ordinary* retriever!'

'Eh?' said Newbugs.

'Look,' went on Sherlock, pointing. 'Two hind feet. Front left foot. Where's the front right? Ah-ha! A three-legged retriever, Newbugs!'

But if he was expecting a pat on the back for this piece of shrewd observation, he was to be disappointed. Newbugs actually began to giggle, barely able to contain the surprise he was about to launch upon his friend. 'How many legs have I got?' he said, almost bursting.

Sherlock who knew he was walking into a trap could only answer: 'Two.'

Newbugs immediately lifted one of them, and began hopping about on the other. 'And how many prints am I making?' he asked fairly roaring with laughter now.

'A four-legged dog that walks on three legs?' puzzled Sherlock. 'But why?'

'I've know'd a fox do it,' said Newbugs. 'He had a thorn in his paw!' and once again he burst into barely controllable laughter.

'A dog with a thorn in his paw . . .' mused Sherlock.

But what dog? What had it been doing at the hut? And what, if anything, was the significance of its having had a thorn in its paw? If, indeed, that's why it had been walking three-legged, as Newbugs had suggested. He would have to look out for this dog. It should not be too hard to find. Labrador retrievers were by no means common in those parts.

4

Tea at the Manor House

The following afternoon punctually at three-thirty a
carriage drew up outside Aunt Rachel's front gate. It
had been despatched by Colonel Turnbull to collect
Aunt Rachel's party and to convey them to the Manor
House for four o'clock tea.

Inside the little house, all was still in pandemonium,
as it had been ever since the delivery of the invitation
the previous day. There was just one small haven of
calm, and that was Sherlock's room. Aunt Rachel had
been most displeased when Sherlock, on being
informed of the honour that had been conferred upon
them all, had suggested that the Turnbulls must be 'up
to something', and thenceforth there had been no
communication between the boy and his Aunt other
than a terse instruction to 'make sure he looked
presentable.' To this end, old Doctor Sowerbutts had
actually given him a new hat. Sherlock knew well
enough the hot water he'd find himself in should he
appear in his old billycock. And the doctor, informed
of his plight, had fished about in a desk drawer and
come up with a never-yet-worn tweed cap that had
been sent him the previous year by a friend in
Scotland. It was, he said, though not to his liking, in
the very latest fashion. It had peaks front and back and
ear flaps which, when not in use, could be tied above
the crown. It was of the sort much favoured by
gentlemen stalking deer in the Highlands. Sherlock
fancied he looked pretty dapper in it.

So now, finally, the front door opened and out they all trooped.

What a sight for sore eyes they were! Aunt Rachel was covered from head to toe in ribbons. Her hat streamed ribbons; her bodice cascaded ribbons; her skirt was festooned with ribbons. As she swept down the garden path she looked like a man-o'-war dressed overall. Her justification for this extravagance was that she was 'helping the poor ribbon-makers of Coventry.' Behind her came Brother Gideon buttoned into a black suit tight and shiny as a grape. And next, with Mrs Cunliffe still fussing about her, there emerged Charity, lacy as a doily and puffed up like a pouter pigeon. Last of all, and embarrassed beyond words, came Sherlock, trying to look as inconspicuous as possible. It was a task rendered the more difficult by Aunt Rachel's determination that the entire village should be aware that it was they who were riding in the Colonel's carriage. To this end she spent the best part of five minutes 'arranging' them on their seats like dolls in a toy-shop window that they might be clearly visible from the outside. Thus 'arranged' they eventually set out for the Manor House.

The carriage bowled through the village at a trot, Aunt Rachel and Gideon and Charity waving extravagantly to the merest acquaintances and even, on one occasion, to two complete strangers, militiamen recruiting, who looked surprised but nevertheless saluted smartly much to the delight of the carriage party.

Soon they were clear of the village and out in the country, passing between autumn hedgerows rich in the red berries of dog rose and holly, and fields brown and fallow. Not many minutes later the carriage turned in through the great iron gates of the Manor House itself.

The tall Indian known as Ranjeet opened the front door to the party and ushered them into the Drawing Room where they were formally welcomed by Colonel Turnbull and his wife. Mrs Turnbull did not rise from the chaise-longue on which she sat languidly, a pet spaniel nestled up beside her.

'We would have extended an invitation long before this, Mrs Holmes,' she said wearily to Aunt Rachel. 'But I am afraid I am unable to entertain as much as I would wish.'

'My wife suffers from poor health, alas,' confirmed the Colonel. 'The Indian climate didn't suit her at all.'

In the next fifteen minutes or so, while tea was poured and passed, and pastries handed round, there was much talk of Mrs Turnbull's poor health, of the decimating effect of the Indian climate, and of the sadness of the events that had befallen the Holmeses, Sherlock in particular. Aunt Rachel twittered on each subject in turn; and Brother Gideon chimed 'Indeed! Indeed!' at intervals (and stuffed his face between times as if he'd not eaten for a week); and Charity sat on the edge of her chair eyeing the grand piano greedily, eager to play and sing, having announced that she could and would, and having been promised by Mrs Turnbull that she should – but later.

Sherlock, cup and saucer in hand, wandered to the window. He was aware that Ranjeet was watching him like a cat. And he noticed that the Indian constantly toyed with a handsomely initialled gold ring that he wore on his signet finger.

Sherlock was puzzled by Mrs Turnbull. Could this seemingly sickly creature have been the woman who had run so fleetingly from the lawn that first day he was back? There were moments when the turn of her head, or a sudden arm movement reminded him very strongly of the figure on the garden seat. But for much of the time there seemed no similarity whatever. But if the woman on the lawn was *not* Mrs Turnbull, then who was she? More importantly, perhaps, *where* was she?

Sherlock was pondering these questions when the door opened and there entered the person he had most looked forward to meeting that day, the fair-haired arrogant youth who had set the wolf-hound on him. He was accompanied by a tall, thin, moustachioed army officer of about thirty.

'Ah!' said the Colonel, 'My nephew, Jasper Moran. And Captain Cholmondeley, who is seconded to the garrison at Fulwood Barracks, Preston. Gentlemen, I'd like you to meet Mrs Holmes and her family.'

The two young men proceeded to greet each of the visitors in turn. 'Jasper is at University,' continued the Colonel as the introductions progressed. 'He is staying with us only until his brother Sebastian returns from India in a few weeks times. He's in the Army out there. Runs in the family, d'you see!'

'Which is why I have no compunction in regularly approaching the Colonel for subscriptions to military charities,' said Captain Cholmondeley, with a horsey laugh.

'He pesters me continually!' said the Colonel.

Gideon, carried away by the spirit of the moment, said suddenly: 'I have a cousin in the service. You are most welcome to approach *me* at any time, Captain. At any time at all. My card.' And he flourished his card-case.

By this time, Jasper Moran, in his circulating, had come face to face with Sherlock.

'*We've* met before,' said Sherlock coolly.

'Yes, I know,' drawled Jasper, with studied politeness. 'So sorry I set the dog on you. I thought you were one of the village lads, poking about out there. We are plagued by poachers.'

'You must be,' said Sherlock drily, 'if they come in broad daylight with portmanteaux in their hands.'

Colonel Turnbull, trying to de-fuse the situation, exclaimed 'Fair point! Jasper can be a little over-hasty, I'm afraid,' and Sherlock noticed that he glanced warningly at Jasper.

But Uncle Gideon was having none of it. 'Sherlock had no right to be there,' he piped. 'No right at all. I told him so at the time. I said ''you have no right to be there''. I am well enough versed in the laws of trespass. The law is my profession. Perhaps, Colonel, I might leave *you* my card?' and he flourished his card-case again.

It was at this point that Mrs Turnbull decided to ask Charity to sing. She was led to the pianoforte by Captain Cholmondeley, and there was a good deal of palaver over the piano stool. It was too low for her. So Captain Cholmondeley raised it. It was now too high for her. So Captain Cholmondeley lowered it again. It was then too far from the keyboard. Captain Cholmondeley moved it a little closer. But then Charity was unable to squeeze between it and the piano. So, the gallant Captain, all eyes upon him now, moved it back again, helped the young lady onto it, and then lifted stool *and* young lady into the perfect position, amid light applause from the company. Charity was loving every minute of it. There was a moment's pause, and then she announced primly: 'Absent Friends.' She hit the piano a mighty thwack and began.

45

'And she says she can play the piano better than I play the violin!' said Sherlock quietly to Jasper.

Jasper said innocently, 'Well, can she?'

Charity now proceeded to caterwaul her way through a repertoire which, in addition to 'Absent Friends,' included 'I'm a Poor Shepherd Maid,' 'Till Doomed for Him to Languish,' 'My Mother's Bible,' and 'The Captive Greek Girl.' By the time she came to announce her final piece, Gideon's plate, which he had taken the precaution of piling high with food as she had started, was empty. What's more, his head kept nodding forward onto his chest, and his eyes kept dropping shut. Each time they did so Aunt Rachel, uncannily aware, rammed a bony elbow into his ribs and he jolted awake again, always with an ill-timed shout of 'Bravo!'

When it was at last all over and fresh tea had been brought, Jasper again approached Sherlock. 'I hear it was you who found the body of that tramp in the woods,' he said.

Ah! So here, perhaps, was the reason for their unexpected invitation!

'He was not a tramp,' corrected Sherlock. 'He was a running patterer.'

'I'm afraid *I* wouldn't know the difference,' said Jasper.

'Ah well, I would,' said Sherlock finally. 'You see I find all people fascinating, regardless of their station in life. You might say I make a study of human behaviour.'

'Do you now!' Jasper laughed. 'And do you really find *that* sort of human behaviour worthy of serious study?'

'Infinitely!' said Sherlock, pointedly.

46

'Tell me,' went on Jasper, 'does the name Professor James Moriarty mean anything to you?'

'Not a thing. Should it?' asked Sherlock.

'He only happens to be – among other things – the world's greatest living authority on the binomial theorem,' Jasper continued, adding with a self-satisfied grin, '*I* have had the honour of studying under him.'

'Have you?' said Sherlock. 'And tell me, do you find the binomial theorem a subject worthy of serious study?'

'I would have thought it self-evident, Mr Holmes,' said Jasper reprovingly, 'that a theorem propounded by Sir Isaac Newton and subject to a treatise by Professor Moriarty was worthy of serious study. Perhaps you should consider devoting some of your own time to glancing at it. Though I should, perhaps, warn you that it is somewhat more difficult to master than patterer's cant!' and he turned, and would have swept off, but he was foiled by Charity who was standing right behind him.

'Do you dance?' she said.

'Yes,' said Jasper, adding quickly, 'But *never* at teatime.'

'*I* dance,' said Charity, with a coy giggle.

'Almost as well as she plays the piano,' said Sherlock, and he moved away leaving Jasper to his fate. He stopped to have a few words with Mrs Turnbull and made much of patting and talking to her dog. Colonel Turnbull stood at the window, apparently staring out over the lawns. Darkness had settled over the countryside now, and patches of low mist hung about among the trees. As Sherlock came up behind the Colonel, he saw passing outside, and clearly visible in the light of the oil lamps, an Indian servant. He was leading the Irish wolf-hound and another dog, a red-setter, towards the woods.

'You have more dogs out there, I perceive, Colonel,' said Sherlock. The Colonel started at the unexpected closeness of the voice. 'Yes,' he said quietly.

'You have a lot of dogs?'

'Just the three,' replied the Colonel. 'Those two out there and the wife's spaniel. Not like in India.' At that moment the sound of horses was heard. 'Ah, Mrs Holmes,' said the Colonel. 'Your carriage! Well, hasn't the afternoon flown!'

Gideon, popping up to grab a last cake from the plate, said with great sadness '*Tempus edax rerum*, Colonel. Time, the devourer of things!' And he popped the cake into his mouth.

Everybody now said goodbye to everybody else. Charity said good-bye to Jasper Moran and Captain Cholmondeley no less than three times, it might even have been four. Aunt Rachel fawned over the Colonel, and Gideon over his wife. Sherlock's good-byes were polite but brief. He wanted to be gone.

As they passed out of the front door Sherlock somehow or other managed to drop his hat. Not only that, but in trying to pick it up he succeeded in kicking it down the stone steps. Refusing the assistance of a servant, he ran after it himself, to the mortification of Aunt Rachel and Gideon, and actually got down on his hands and knees in the drive and crawled almost to the shrubbery to get it.

As a result there was a frosty silence in the carriage as it pulled away from the front of the house. He *had* disgraced them after all!

'*On* his hands and knees!' wailed Gideon, shaking his head from side to side. 'Like a mudlark!'

On the steps Jasper stood smiling broadly, and Sherlock, raising a hand, waved his fingers at him and smiled back.

There was to be one more disturbance. It came as the carriage was approaching the gates on the way out. Suddenly, Sherlock, shouting that he needed air, lowered the window and stuck his head out. Both Aunt Rachel and Charity shrieked at the sudden inrush of cold air, and Gideon began shivering and making a 'brrrrrrrrr' noise like a clockwork toy.

Precisely at the moment when the carriage passed through the gates, Sherlock pulled his head back in again. And his hat, catching on the window-frame, fell off into the roadway. He shouted for the carriage to stop. Gideon, countermanding his order, shouted for it to proceed. 'Confound the boy's hat! If he can't take better care of it, he don't deserve a hat!' But Aunt Rachel, perceiving that it might very well fall to her to buy a new hat should the old one be lost, insisted that it be retrieved. So, the carriage was duly stopped and Sherlock stepped down to retrieve it. He walked back, taking one of the carriage lamps to light his path. Although he knew precisely where the hat lay, he made much of having to look about for it, and took the opportunity of examining the two great columns that supported the Manor House gates. 'Ah-ha!' he muttered after a while. 'Just as I thought!' Then, sweeping his hat up from the road and slapping it back on his head, he walked jauntily back to the carriage.

As it pulled away, he was whistling a merry tune through his teeth.

'Oh shut up!' snapped Gideon. And it was in silence that they completed the journey home. But Sherlock was exhilarated, and he slept little that night.

5

The Gypsy Calls Again

Next morning, Sherlock was up early, intending to slip down to see the doctors as soon as possible. They were the only people in whom he could confide. But what with one thing and another, it was after lunch before he was able to escape from Aunt Rachel's. By about three o'clock, however, he was sprawled in a chair at the surgery and in full flight about the events of the previous day.

'So why is Colonel Turnbull concealing a dog?' he said, with the air of a man who has just produced a rabbit from his hat.

'What on earth do you mean?' asked John Whitney.

'He admits to having only three dogs,' Sherlock went on, 'a wolf-hound, a spaniel (his wife's lap-dog), and his own gun-dog, a red-setter. Yet, unless I am very much mistaken this hair, which I took the opportunity of removing from the clothing of Mrs Turnbull will, under your microscope, prove to belong to a black Labrador retriever.'

'Good God!' exclaimed George Sowerbutts. 'How do you know that, young'un?'

'Because Newbugs pointed out to me that the tracks about the hut were those of a retriever, and when I so carelessly dropped my hat yesterday, I noticed similar tracks on the ground at the front of the Manor House. Therefore, there is somewhere a retriever. Now, that hair is obviously black. And as the wolf-hound is grey, and both the spaniel and the setter are brown, a process of deduction indicates that the black hair is from the dog I did not see – in other words, the retriever. Hence, for some reason, the Colonel would appear to be concealing a black retriever. Now, why?'

No one had the foggiest notion.

'Furthermore,' continued Sherlock, 'I think you will find that *this* hair is from the same black dog,' and he handed another one across.

'And where did this one come from, then?' asked John Whitney, taking it.

'From Natty Dan's trouser leg. I took it the morning I found him. But, there is something else . . .'

The others looked at each other resignedly.

'According to Sergeant Grimshaw, the people at the Manor House sent Natty packing. Yet, when I examined the gate posts yesterday I found this sign freshly chalked on one of them.' And he drew a 'V' on a piece of paper with a second but inverted 'V' immediately above it. 'It's the patterer's symbol to those who follow indicating "a good house" – "Bone" in their language. Now, Natty might lie to us, but *never* to his friends on the road.'

'So you think the Turnbulls lied to Sergeant Grimshaw about not inviting him in?' said Charlotte.

'I do, indeed,' Sherlock replied. 'But there is something even more curious. 'On both gate-posts, recently scratched, and obviously by various hands, there are numerous signs like this one.' And he drew a simple square. 'Again, a patterer's symbol. But this one means "Gammy" – "likely to have you taken up" – by the law, of course. A warning. A bad house. Now why, if it were normally a bad house for itinerants should it turn out to be such a good one for Natty Dan? What was so special about Natty?'

And without waiting for a reply, he rose from his chair, and strode from the room and from the house.

'Deuced extraordinary lad!' said old Sowerbutts, after he'd gone.

'Strange, indeed,' agreed Whitney, settling to the microscope on his work-bench. And then to Charlotte, 'Shouldn't you have told him that you'd had word from the Grandmother?'

'I suppose I should have done,' said Charlotte. 'I just didn't have the heart.'

Sherlock's Grandmother, his mother's mother, was French and lived in Paris. She was the sister of the well-known artist Horace Vernet, who'd died some nine years previously. She had on occasion visited Pendargh and had struck up a firm friendship with Charlotte Whitney. The two of them corresponded regularly. It was to the grandmother that the Holmeses had fled earlier that year. But the most recent letter to Charlotte had indicated that they were now 'travelling somewhere in Europe' with no intention, it seemed, of returning to England in the forseeable future. They had recently been joined in their journeying by Sherlock's brother Mycroft. So, Sherlock, it appeared, was doomed to remain at Aunt Rachel's.

'I'd *not* tell him if I were you,' said old Sowerbutts. 'Not at all. You know what those Holmeses are like, up and down like corks in a whirlpool!'

'Perhaps you're right, Uncle,' said Charlotte. 'Perhaps it would be best.'

Just then, John Whitney, looking up from the microscope, said: 'You know, George, these hairs *are* from the same animal; I'd say a black retriever.'

'Good Heavens!' said Sowerbutts. 'You don't think there's anything in it, do you?'

'I've no idea,' said Whitney. 'But it certainly looks as if he's right about the dog. And why should the Colonel be hiding it?'

That was the very question that was occupying Sherlock's mind as he walked the woods that late afternoon, having come from the doctors' too restless to return to the claustrophobic atmosphere of Aunt Rachel's prim little house.

So preoccupied was he, that he didn't even notice the gypsy man who suddenly appeared ahead of him. But the gypsy saw Sherlock and immediately vanished into the undergrowth. He watched Sherlock pass him, then stepped onto the path again and began to follow. It was this same gypsy who, shortly afterwards, when darkness had fallen, arrived at the Manor House carrying on his shoulder an unwieldy object wrapped in a blanket.

About ten minutes later Newbugs, setting his snares in the woods, saw the gypsy. He was bending over and covering something with bracken and leaves. After a few minutes he straightened up, looked about him, and strode off. Newbugs moved silently to the spot where he had been. There he saw, sticking out from under the bracken, a pair of black-shoed feet. He dropped his snares and ran pell-mell for the village. He made straight for Aunt Rachel's, and arriving, began hammering on the front door with both fists and shouting, 'Sherlock! Sherlock!'

Above him, a window was flung open and Aunt Rachel's head popped out. 'You just clear off you good-for-nothing little varmit,' she shrieked. 'Sherlock is not here!' And her head popped back in again, and the window slammed shut.

'A body, Missus!' bellowed Newbugs from below. 'Another body! Another body in the woods!'

The window was flung open again. 'What?' shrieked Aunt Rachel. By now windows were opening all around, and all manner of heads were popping out of them.

It was into this commotion, back from visiting a farmer's child who had gone down with the whooping-cough, that John Whitney arrived. And it was not very long afterwards that Newbugs led him and the police sergeant back to where the body lay.

'There! Look! There!' shouted Newbugs, pointing.

'Alright, stand away, you,' said Grimshaw, waving him aside with his lantern. 'Let the dog see the rabbit.' And he began removing the bracken in the region of the face. Even he was surprised by what he found. 'Good Heavens, sir!' he said, straightening up and turning to John Whitney who stood a pace or two behind him. 'It's that boy Holmes!'

It was indeed Sherlock who lay there, immobile, pale, his eyes closed. John Whitney, horrified, stepped forward. He was about to bend over the body when suddenly its eyes opened and Sherlock sat up. 'It really won't do, Sergeant,' he said, looking at Grimshaw. 'Where is the obsequial eloquence in "Good 'eavens! It's that boy 'olmes''!' and he actually gave a passable imitation of the Yorkshireman.

John Whitney was too angry even to be relieved. 'What in Heaven's name are you playing at!' he shouted. Newbugs, laughing, tried to slip away, but Grimshaw grabbed him by the scruff of the neck. 'Oh no you don't!' said the equally angry policeman. 'It's

54

taken a pair of you to rig this trick, and that's for certain.'

'No,' said Sherlock, getting up. 'No, I assure you, sergeant, he had no part in my little deception. I will show you what *he* found.' And from behind a nearby tree he produced a tailor's dummy. It was clothed in full evening dress. 'Here, Sergeant, is your body,' said Sherlock handing it over.

'Well, is *this* what you brought us out here for?' said John Whitney, turning angrily to Newbugs.

'*I* didn't know, sir!' squealed the boy. 'It looked like a stiff'un, sir! Honest, it did!'

'Ah well,' said Grimshaw. 'A simple lost or stolen by the look of it. Gypsies!' and he sniffed deprecatingly.

'Well, do cheer up, John,' said Sherlock to Whitney. 'You should be delighted that I am, after all, still in the land of the living.'

'To be perfectly truthful,' said Whitney, 'I am not altogether certain that I am!'

And he and the sergeant turned on their heels and strode off through the dark woods, the light from the sergeant's bulls-eye lantern bobbing ahead of them like a will-o'-the-wisp.

Newbugs and Sherlock looked at each other sheepishly and shrugged.

When Sherlock arrived home at about six-thirty that evening he found everybody dressed up to the nines and sitting, angry and fidgety, in the parlour. Did he not remember that they were all due at a concert in Longridge at seven? No, he didn't.

They all tutted and shook their heads. Where had he been? What had he been up to? And when he told them they were even angrier.

'A stupid prank, boy!' said Gideon, almost shouting. 'Infantile! Ghoulish *and* infantile! And *not* funny!'

'My sentiments exactly,' said Aunt Rachel.

'Obstructing Sergeant Grimshaw!' squawked Gideon, almost bursting a blood vessel.

'I would never have told you,' said Sherlock, 'but for the fact that I considered honesty would, in this house, be the best policy.'

The attackers fell momentarily silent.

'As indeed it is, boy! As indeed it is!' said Gideon rallying. 'As indeed it *is*, and *was*, and *ever shall be*!'

'We are none of us, I hope, implying that you were wrong to tell the truth, Sherlock, my dear,' said Aunt Rachel following her brother's lead. 'You were, of course, perfectly right.'

'Indeed! Indeed!' chimed Gideon. 'Credit where credit's due! 'Nuff said!'

Charity was obviously very disappointed that it was all over.

'Now you'd best hurry yourself, boy,' said Gideon. 'The concert commences at seven.'

But Sherlock, professing a terrible headache and the probable onset of influenza, begged to be excused, and the party set off in a hired cab amid much tutting.

Sherlock spent the early part of his evening lying on his bed pondering events. Was the dummy of any significance? Why had it been dumped? Such things were usually stolen for the clothes they carried, but the clothes had been dumped as well. It did not make sense.

He placed his hands behind his head, stretched out, and closed his eyes. Then, from below, he heard drifting the sound of a concertina, and a man's voice, singing:

56

'I've travelled about a bit in my time
And of troubles I've seen a few.
But found it better in ev'ry clime
To paddle my own canoe . . .'

Sherlock sat up, listening. The voice continued:

'My wants are small, I care not at all
If my debts are paid when due;
I drive away strife in the ocean of life
While I paddle my own canoe.'

Sherlock rose from the bed, left his room, and wandered down the stairs and towards the kitchen, from whence the music was coming. He opened the kitchen door a fraction, and peered in. On one side of the kitchen range, with her back to him, sat Mrs Cunliffe, knitting. On the other side sat a tall, well-built and ruggedly nice-looking man of about forty who was wearing a uniform which Sherlock recognised at once as being that of a Guard on the London & North Western Railway.

As the door opened, the man looked up, and seeing Sherlock at once stopped playing. This caused Mrs Cunliffe to turn her head, and at the unexpected sight of Sherlock she leapt to her feet. 'Oh! Mr Sherlock!' she said. 'I thought the whole family was out at the concert.'

'All but me, Mrs Cunliffe,' he said. And then, indicating the railwayman, 'Well, aren't you going to introduce us?'

The railwayman, who had also risen to his feet, now stepped forward with a hand outstretched. 'Tom Hudson, sir. 'Ow d'you do. I've 'eard a deal about yer from me little Liza Ann, 'ere. Full of you, she is.'

'Tom!' said Mrs Cunliffe, in gentle rebuke, 'know your place! Of course, Mr Sherlock, he don't normally make hisself at home in my kitchen like this.'

'I know the missus don't like followers,' said Hudson, with the air of a man who intended to continue following whether she did or not.

'You never told me there was someone, Mrs Cunliffe,' said Sherlock smiling at her. 'Secrets, eh?'

Mrs Cunliffe said, very confidentially, 'Mr Hudson is the first man as has took my fancy since my poor dear Jack was killed in India, all them years ago.'

'Well, I'll not intrude,' said Sherlock, and was about to leave, but Mrs Cunliffe took hold of his arm and led him to the fire. 'You just sit yourself down, and welcome. How about a nice cup of tea, eh?'

'Oh thank you, Mrs Cunliffe. That would be nice,' said Sherlock. And he sat; and Hudson sat; and Mrs Cunliffe poured tea; and the domestic scene was re-established with Sherlock now a part of it. 'Well, do play,' he said to Tom. 'I liked the song. That's why I came down.'

Hudson, taking up the concertina, sang:

> 'Then love your neighbour as yourself
> As the world you go travelling through . . .'

Mrs Cunliffe joined in the final two lines of the chorus:

> 'And never sit down with a tear or a frown
> But paddle your own canoe!'

'I heard Harry Clifton hisself sing that song, when he come to the Corn Exchange in Preston last year,' said Mrs Cunliffe, to Sherlock.

'Ah, Liza Ann,' said Tom Hudson. 'When you

become Mrs Hudson and come to live with me in my cosy little house in London, we shall visit all the music-halls in town – the Alhambra, the Canterbury, the Oxford, the Old Mo . . .'

'The Old Mo!' exclaimed Sherlock.

'The Middlesex Music Hall, Mr Holmes,' explained the guard. 'Drury Lane. Used at one time to be the Mogul Saloon, and some'ow the nick-name stuck.'

'Haybag Old Mo!' said Sherlock, recalling Natty Dan's last message. 'So that's it! Haybag – a woman. Old Mo – a Music Hall. A woman at a Music Hall! I think I see what Natty Dan was trying to tell me, at last! Thanks Tom!' and he rushed from the kitchen.

Mrs Cunliffe and Tom Hudson stared after him. 'What *did* I say?' said Hudson.

Mrs Cunliffe shook her head and shrugged.

6

The Riddle of the Dummies

At eleven o'clock the following morning a large horse-drawn van might have been seen heading up the drive towards the Manor House. On its side was sedately lettered 'H. McTaggart. Photographer. Great Avenham Street, Preston.'

These were still the days of wet-plate photography and the van, apart from containing all the photographer's paraphernalia, was also a travelling dark-room.

The driver was a tall, slim man of indeterminate age, with a ruddy complexion, bright red hair and wild red whiskers.

On arrival at the Manor House he announced himself as Hamish McTaggart, come to photograph the Turnbulls on behalf of the Lord Lieutenant of the County who was in the process of compiling a photographic record of Lancashire's notable families. After some disputation with Ranjeet, for there appeared to have been a mix-up over the appointment, and his arrival was not in fact expected, he was finally admitted to the house where, in the next hour or so, he secured a series of studies of Colonel and Mrs Turnbull, Jasper and their servants.

Later that same day on a chair in McTaggart's studio in Preston, there lay not only McTaggart's hat, and cloak, and suit, but also his hair and whiskers.

'Where *did* you get those dreadful whiskers?' said *Hector* McTaggart, the *real* H. McTaggart, Photographer. 'When you said you proposed passing your-self off as a cousin of mine, you no said you'd be wearing those dreadful things!'

'They happen to be the only ones I have,' said Sherlock, wiping the last vestiges of his 'ruddy complexion' away with a cloth. 'Wigs and whiskers are expensive.' The McTaggart laughed. 'Well, I'll say this for you, you're no a bad photographer. If you're ever in need of a position . . .'

Sherlock had known this amiable McTaggart ever since, at the age of five or six, he had been taken to Great Avenham Street dressed in a white sailor suit to be photographed against a nine-foot-square backdrop of ironclads anchored off Spithead. McTaggart had then been a young man of twenty-two, newly come to town, and the patronage of the Holmeses had done much to establish the success of his business. It was from him, subsequently, over the years, that Sherlock had acquired his knowledge of photography.

He now wrote a brief note which he slipped, together with one of his photographs, into a large envelope, addressing this to 'Mr T. Hudson, Guard, London & North Western Railway Company, c/o Euston Station.'

'Thanks for everything, Hector,' he said, heading for the door.

'Aye, you're most welcome, lad. Though I'd dearly love to know what it is you're up to!' shouted the McTaggart after him as he sped from the shop in the direction of the station. Here, he handed the envelope to an official of the railway company who promised to see that it was put on the next down train to London.

The next few days passed very slowly. There was little

61

more he could do until he heard from Tom Hudson. But by the morning of the fourth day, he could stand the inactivity no longer and decided to risk the wrath of Sergeant Grimshaw and drop into the police house to see if anything new had come to light. To his great surprise the Sergeant greeted him affably. 'Hello, lad! And what can I do for you, then?'

'Have you discovered yet where that dummy came from, Sergeant?' he asked.

'Clitheroe', said the sergeant with a rosy smile. 'It came from Clitheroe.'

'But that's miles away,' said Sherlock.

'There's been a spate of them stolen,' volunteered the policeman. 'Six in all have been reported. All over the county. Preston, Darwen, Garstang, Adlington, Rawtenstall, and ours, to be precise.'

'In that order?' asked Sherlock.

Grimshaw glanced through the papers in a file. 'Yes,' he said after a while, 'In that order. And always the same story, lad, gypsies seen in the area. Ours is the only one that's been recovered to date.'

'Well, that's most interesting,' said Sherlock. 'Thank you.' And he was about to leave, when the Sergeant called him back. 'I say, not so fast, lad. Seeing as I've just obliged you with certain information, perhaps you would now be good enough to oblige me.'

Well he needn't think I'm telling him about Old Mo, said Sherlock to himself. But Grimshaw had long since given up looking for Old Mo. He had other things on his mind. 'Your Mrs Cunliffe now?' he said.

'Mrs Cunliffe?' said Sherlock, most surprised. 'What about her?'

'Where's her husband?' asked the Sergeant.

'Oh dead. Long ago. Killed in India,' said Sherlock,

quickly adding, 'nothing suspicious, mind you. He was a soldier.'

'Oh!' said Grimshaw, beaming. 'So she's a widow-woman, then?'

'Exactly!' said Sherlock, totally unable to see where this line of questioning was leading.

'She's a fine-looking woman, your Mrs Cunliffe. A fine looking woman. Can she cook?'

'Excellently,' said Sherlock.

'Oh. That'll be fine then. Just fine. It's most important they can cook. Well, I'm very much obliged to you, Mr Holmes. Good-day to you.'

Sherlock wandered home without the faintest idea of what the Sergeant had been getting at, and more than ever convinced that he was a most peculiar man.

At the precise moment that Sherlock came out of Sergeant Grimshaw's garden gate, events at the Manor House took an unpremeditated turn.

It began simply enough when Colonel Turnbull, who had been sitting in his arm-chair, got up and, carrying a glass, went to the side-board. Jasper was at that time seated in another chair, cleaning his gun. Mrs Turnbull sat upright on the settee, her eyes closed. On a small table in front of her a partly-played game of patience was set out. Apart from the ponderous ticking of the great grandfather clock, the room was silent. Then there came the gentle clink of a glass stopper being removed from a decanter.

'I do wish you'd stop drinking that stuff,' said Jasper without turning.

The Colonel, decanter in one hand, stopper in the other, hesitated for a moment, then replaced the stopper and put the decanter down. 'Very well,' he said. 'I can take it or leave it, you know.' And he returned to his seat. 'It's just the tension,' he went on. 'We're getting close, aren't we?'

'All the more reason not to make mistakes,' said Jasper.

'Meaning?' said the Colonel frostily.

'Turning that dummy away for one thing. That was an extraordinarily silly mistake.'

'Not half as silly as inviting that pedlar fellah in,' said the Colonel angrily. '*That* brought the police sniffing about up here.'

Jasper, leaning his gun against the chair, stood. 'That pedlar' he said, 'provided us with valuable information which we could have acquired in no other way. Anyway, there was not the slightest risk involved. Or wouldn't have been, had you not been drinking that stuff and allowed that damned dog to escape.'

The Colonel rose, too. 'Now just you listen to me, you cocky little whipper-snapper . . .' he shouted at Jasper.

Then Mrs Turnbull, opening her eyes, said wearily from the settee, 'Oh *do* stop arguing, the pair of you. You're getting on my nerves.'

The Colonel, choosing the easier target, swung on her. 'Oh-ho!' he yelled. 'So we're getting on Madame's nerves, are we! Well,' and he bent right over her, red in the face and bullying, '*Madame* shouldn't be lolling about down here listening to us. *Madame* should be back upstairs at work!'

'Work!' said Mrs Turnbull, quiet but tense. 'You talk to me of work!' And the tension that had been building up over a long period now was suddenly released. 'I do more work than any of you!' Her voice grew louder and shriller. 'I work from morning to

64

night, day in and day out, and have done all these months!!' She was now quite hysterical. 'It's *all* work! Nothing *but* work! Work, work, work, work, work, work, work! Until I sometimes think I shall go clear out of my mind!!' And she screamed, a long, high, wailing scream and collapsed back on the settee, tears streaming down her face.

'You damned fool!' shouted Jasper. 'Now look what you've done! Drunk or sober you're a brainless menace!' At that moment the door was flung open and there stood Ranjeet. He clapped his hands imperiously.

'I will not tolerate such unseemly behaviour,' he said. Mrs Turnbull's violent sobbing gradually subsided. 'You will all compose yourselves,' went on the Indian. 'And you will return to your work immediately.' With muttered apologies, Colonel and Mrs Turnbull slipped by him and out of the room. As Jasper reached the door, Ranjeet held up a hand to stop him. 'Mrs Turnbull gives me cause for concern,' he said. 'The strain appears to be telling. And *she* we cannot risk. I suggest you summon the Professor to "re-inspire" her'.

'Very well,' said Jasper meekly. 'I shall see to it.' And he too passed from the room.

The Indian, having shut the door behind them all, moved silently to the window and stared blackly out across the autumnal woods. Once again, from the direction of the Coach House there came the sound of hammering.

Had Ranjeet been able to see deep enough into the woods, he would have seen Sergeant Grimshaw down on his hands and knees picking mushrooms. They were

65

Chanterelles, those bright yellow mushrooms that are common in beech woodlands, and the Sergeant was picking them onto a large red-spotted kerchief. He then gathered the four corners of the kerchief together and was about to knot them when he saw lying just ahead of him, a loop of strong black elastic. Picking it up, he wound it about the top of his bundle.

Some short while later, the Sergeant arrived at Mrs Cunliffe's kitchen, carrying the mushrooms in one hand and a dead rabbit in the other. Spreading these out on the scrubbed table like a market-man laying up his stall, he said hopefully, 'I thought, Mrs Cunliffe, that if I provided the rabbit, you might at some mutually convenient time, agree to provide the pie.'

'You've got a cheek, Sergeant Grimshaw, and that's for sure!' said Mrs Cunliffe, not pausing in her sweeping.

'*And* I brought you these,' he said, opening the kerchief to reveal the mushrooms. 'Picked 'em meself, I did. And nothing better in a rabbit pie, Mrs Cunliffe, believe you me!'

There then came a tap on the kitchen door, which still stood ajar. The door opened and there stood Tom Hudson. Glaring at the policeman, he said, pointedly, 'Am I intruding?'

'Why, Mr Hudson!' said Mrs Cunliffe, setting her broom aside, 'Not at all! Come along in!'

Hudson entered, glaring from Grimshaw to the rabbit and from the mushrooms back to Grimshaw. He beckoned Mrs Cunliffe to him, and said quietly in her ear, 'I wondered if I might have a word with young Sherlock. I've got what he wanted.'

'I'll go and fetch him,' said Mrs Cunliffe. 'You two make yourselves known to each other.' As she left the room the two uniformed men pulled themselves up to their full heights and eyed each other like fighting cocks. 'Alright, then,' said Tom Hudson. 'Who are you?'

When, no more than a few minutes later, Mrs Cunliffe returned with Sherlock, Tom Hudson was standing alone in the kitchen, a self-satisfied look on his face.

'Where's Sergeant Grimshaw?' asked Mrs Cunliffe, looking about her.

'I've seen him off,' said Hudson nonchalantly.

'Oh Tom, you never did!' said Mrs Cunliffe. She was genuinely worried. After all, Sergeant Grimshaw might be a fool and he might be a nuisance, but he *was*, nevertheless, the law!

'I know these perlicemen,' said Tom. 'If they can find a table to get their feet under and a pie to get their teeth into, you're never rid of them. Why, he even had the confounded impudence to refer to you as Cookey!'

'All that man thinks about is food,' smiled Mrs Cunliffe, busying herself at the range.

'Well, Tom,' said Sherlock to Hudson. 'So you got my message alright?'

'Oh, yes,' replied the guard. 'I did exactly as you asked. I took the photograph to the Old Mo and showed it about a bit. They knew her alright. She used to work there.'

'Did she now!' said Sherlock. At last things seemed to be moving.

'Name's Bessie Bright,' continued Hudson. 'Seems she's quite well known in her way, or was. Did monologues, character impersonations, that sort of thing. But she dropped out of sight a couple of years back and hasn't been seen there since.'

67

'Thanks, Tom,' said Sherlock. 'That is most useful.'

'Ere, and another thing,' said Hudson. 'I bumped into an old friend of mine in the village on the way here. Alf Prendergast. He's Station Master at Preston now. Seems he's a regular visitor to the Manor House. Shares an interest in butterflies with your Colonel. Small world, in't it?'

'Butterflies?' said Sherlock. 'Colonel Turnbull?' And then he noticed lying on the kitchen table, the ring of black elastic. 'I say, Mrs Cunliffe,' he said, picking it up. 'Where did this come from?'

Mrs Cunliffe looked up from the saucepan she was stirring on the range. 'That? Oh it was tied round the mushrooms Sergeant Grimshaw brought,' she said. Sherlock looked at them. Chanterelles! Then, examining the elastic, he noticed that set into it was a tiny piece of soft black leather. It was ragged, stained and torn. 'May I have this, Mrs Cunliffe?' he asked.

'Of course,' she said. 'I'd only throw it out.'

'Thanks,' and he headed for the door.

'You're not going out?'

'I must, yes.'

'But Mr Sherlock, they'll all be in for lunch in fifteen minutes or so, and you know how angry they get!'

'I'm sorry, Mrs Cunliffe,' he said, 'But there *are* more pressing things than meals. Make my apologies, will you!' And he shot through the kitchen door and set off, running, down the street.

By the time that Aunt Rachel, Gideon and Charity came to sit down to lunch, the empty place at their table a reminder to them of the burden they had to bear, Sherlock had already brought John Whitney and George Sowerbutts up to date with the events of the

68

previous few days. John Whitney, still cool with him over the affair of the dummy, had been angered yet again by the tale of Hamish McTaggart and the impudent invasion of the Manor House. This anger had in no way been allayed by Sherlock's subsequent revelation that Mrs Turnbull had been known at the Old Mo. However, old George Sowerbutts had found that fact salaciously amusing. 'Well, well! Fancy old Turnbull marrying a gal from the music-hall stage!' he'd laughed. 'The old dog!'

'And if it were true,' said John Whitney coldly, 'it's quite understandable that he should want to keep it quiet. You know what people in these parts would make of it. The Turnbulls would be finished socially.'

'It hardly matters,' said Sherlock. 'But what about this? I devoted some little time this morning to trying to discover if there were any connection between the towns from which the dummies were stolen. And there *is* one, a very significant one. May I have a pencil and a piece of paper, please?'

John Whitney handed him both without a word.

'Now,' he went on. 'Take the initial letters of each of those towns, in order. Preston, Darwen, Garstang, Adlington and Rawtenstall.' And he wrote, spaced at intervals, the letters P- D - G - A - R. 'Then insert two letters between each of them,' he continued, filling in the blank spaces with 'en', 'ar', 'hm', 'no'. 'And what do you have?' He passed the sheet of paper to John Whitney. On it was now written PenDarGhmAnoR. Pendargh Manor. 'The brain behind this is adept at cryptographs,' added Sherlock.

'I say, that's a bit far-fetched,' said John Whitney. 'And in any case, I thought you said that *six* dummies had in all been stolen, the last of them from Clitheroe?'

'Ah-ha!' said George Sowerbutts. 'That puts the kybosh on your cryptograph, young'un!'

'Not at all,' insisted Sherlock. 'It leads me to believe that the last one was a mistake and was rejected, which would explain why it was abandoned in the woods. But we shall very soon see. Doctor Sowerbutts, may I borrow your telescope?'

'By all means,' said the Doctor. 'Now let me think, where did I last see that?'

'It's hanging in the hall!' said Sherlock. He abruptly left the room, taking the old naval telescope from its place on the wall, he let himself out of the house and headed towards the woods.

Once under the bare trees, Sherlock scouted his way towards the Manor House, and having drawn as close as he considered advisable, he looked round for a suitable vantage point. He finally chose a large old oak, standing about twenty feet in from the Manor House lands. Shinning up, he perched himself in the fork of two high branches and settled down to observe the house. There was no activity to be seen anywhere about. The Coach House was shut tight and silent; the grounds were deserted. He trained the glass one by one on the windows of the house. Nothing. It was like a house of the dead.

The time seemed to pass extraordinarily slowly. Twilight came and then the dark. It was a black night, and a chilly one. Sherlock was glad of his deer-stalker's hat and pulled the flaps down about his ears. The only sound, apart from the wind sighing in the trees, was that of the occasional night-bird. After a while, his legs began to feel horribly cramped, but despite his discomfort he determined to maintain his vigil.

Then, suddenly, it began. A light appeared at a window on the first floor. It grew gradually brighter and brighter. Putting the telescope to his eye, Sherlock could see two Indians placing lighted candles and candelabra about the room. Inside, he could see five figures. Standing talking to them was Mrs Turnbull.

Then, below him, he heard a whispered voice. 'Sherlock! Sherlock! Where are you?' It was John Whitney. Sherlock pulled a large piece of bark from a dead bough above him and dropped it onto Whitney's head. Whitney looked up, startled. 'Sherlock? What in Heaven's name are you doing up there? Your Aunt Rachel is frantic with worry. She sent Mrs Cunliffe, and Charlotte sent me! You're to come home at once!'

'Come up, John,' said Sherlock, ignoring his pleas. 'Just for a minute. You must!'

After some protestation, Whitney laboriously climbed up and was handed the telescope. 'In there,' said Sherlock, 'you will find the answer to your missing tradesmen's dummies, John.'

Whitney put the glass to his eye. In the room, Mrs Turnbull now sat at the head of a table fully set for dinner. The Indian servants were waiting on her. The only other 'guests' at the table were the dummies. At the foot of the table stood Ranjeet, and against the sideboard leaned Jasper Moran.

'Good Heavens!' said Whitney. 'What *is* going on?'

But Sherlock merely gave him an inscrutable smile and taking the telescope back resumed his observation. From now on he was going to impart no information until he was certain that he had sufficient data to justify his conclusions.

Two hours later Mrs Turnbull was still seated at the

dinner table; dinner was still being served; and she was still eating it. Outside, perched uncomfortably in their tree, Sherlock and John Whitney were still watching. Jasper had by this time slumped into a chair. But Ranjeet still stood at the end of the table. He held a pocket-watch in his hand,

'No, no, no!' he said. 'You are still not fast enough. You have exactly half-an-hour. Not a minute more. Soup, fish, sirloin of beef, and dessert in half-an-hour. We will try it once more.' And he signalled the servants to begin again.

But Mrs Turnbull slammed her knife and fork down on the table. 'Look 'ere, dearie,' she said in defiantly broad Cockney. 'I can't eat another bloomin' fing!'

'This is no time to lose your appetite, Mrs Turnbull!' said Ranjeet menacingly. 'We will do it again!'

'Look, you can do what you bloomin' well like, duckie,' said Mrs Turnbull standing. 'But like I've told yer, dearies, *I've* 'ad enough!' And raising an arm she swiped the head off the dummy seated next to her. It rolled off its body and across the floor. Ranjeet stared at it with a mixture of anger, impatience, and desperation. But just then, from outside, there came the sound of a rider approaching. Jasper leapt to the window and peered into the night. The sound drew closer. 'It's alright,' he said, 'I think the Professor has arrived!'

From their observation post at the top of the tree, Sherlock and John Whitney watched as the muffled rider, dressed entirely in black, galloped to the front of the House, dismounted, and disappeared inside.

As the front door closed behind him, the clock above the stables chimed midnight.

7

A Singular Thorn

For young Sherlock and John Whitney there was little
else to see that night, though they maintained their
vigil for several more hours. Shortly after the arrival of
the horseman, the candles in the room they had been
observing were extinguished, though elsewhere in the
house lights burned late behind closed shutters.

The Professor was closeted with Mrs Turnbull for
the best part of three hours. Throughout that time
Jasper Moran waited in the corridor outside her room.
Several times, he heard her shout 'I can't! I can't!'
And each time the solemn, patient, almost mesmeric
voice of the Professor had loudly insisted 'You *can*. You
must. And you *shall*!'

Below, in the great Drawing Room, Colonel
Turnbull paced the floor. 'Do you really think she will
be capable of seeing this through?' he asked Ranjeet at
one point.

'I am quite certain she will,' Ranjeet replied. 'You
forget, Colonel, that our Mrs Turnbull is a professional
performer. She lives on her nerves. And I am quite
sure the Professor will be able to inspire in her that
combination of dedication and egoism that will ensure
"a good performance on the night", as she might say.'

'Hm. I hope you're right,' said the Colonel. 'There
is a great deal of money at stake.'

No one, not even Jasper, ever learned what passed
between Mrs Turnbull and the Professor in the locked
room during those long and difficult hours of the night,
but when she finally re-emerged her confidence was fully

restored, her dedication resurgent, her energy renewed.

There was a good deal of general relief and a desire for rest, but, tired as they all were, nobody at the Manor House was to get much sleep that night. Within an hour-and-a-half of the Professor's departure, and still before dawn, another Indian arrived at the house. This man was the Munshi (the word, as Colonel Turnbull explained to his wife was Urdu and meant simply a native language teacher or secretary). The Munshi came with instructions from the Professor that Mrs Turnbull was to be subjected, without further delay, to a series of the most rigorous tests and examinations. Thus, well before six o'clock, having cat-napped for a mere thirty-five minutes or so, Mrs Turnbull was back at work.

Apart from the Munshi himself, the only person present throughout her examination was Ranjeet. But when, towards the end of it, Jasper and the Colonel were summoned, all seemed to be going even better than anyone had dared to hope. As Jasper and the Colonel entered the room Mrs Turnbull was sitting, somewhat formally, in an arm-chair. All trace of her cockney accent had now vanished and she answered the Munshi's questions unhesitatingly in clear and ringing tones.

'Fruit?'

'Oranges and pears.'

'Apples?'

'Oh yes. Very large indigestible apples.'

'Games?'

'Cards, chess, draughts . . .'

'And do you prefer the house to be hot or cold?'

'Oh cold. All doctors say that heat is unwholesome, but cold is wholesome.'

74

'Good. You are familiar with the works of Felix Mendelssohn?'

'Yes.'

'Are there any of his songs that have an especial appeal for you?'

'The Pilgerspruch "Lass dich nur". I can even sing you one written by his sister Fanny, "Schoner und Schoner schmuckt sich!"'

Then, suddenly speaking German, the Munshi asked, 'You have, of course, visited Germany?'

Mrs Turnbull, in equally fluent German replied: 'Indeed, yes. Cologne. Bruhl. Bonn. They had just erected the statue of Beethoven there.'

The Munshi put the next question in French. 'You have also visited France?' he asked.

Mrs Turnbull's French, too, was fluent. 'Mais oui! Paris, Versailles. It was in August, I remember'—all this in French, of course—'There was a ball. I can even tell you what I wore. A white dress, a white silk hat, with a mantilla and a parasol of green.'

The Munshi, apparently satisfied, then carried out a series of physical tests, asking Mrs Turnbull to stand; to sit; to turn her head this way and that; to raise and lower an arm; and finally to rise and walk towards the door. She had almost reached the door when he said commandingly, 'Turn! Come towards me!' Mrs Turnbull did so. He approached her, smiling, and somewhere about the centre of the room they met. She, obviously pleased with the way things were going, returned his smile. Then, suddenly, before anyone knew what was happening, he raised his arm and crashed the flat of his hand into the side of her face. Jasper and Colonel Turnbull gasped. But Mrs Turnbull didn't so much as flinch. Her face calm and controlled, and showing no emotion, she said, without raising her voice: 'How dare you! What in Heaven's name do you think you are doing?'

The smile returned to the Munshi's face. 'Excellent! Excellent!' he said. Then, turning to Ranjeet, 'Her command of the languages is truly amazing. To have become so fluent in so short a time . . .'

'She has a natural ear,' replied Ranjeet 'The gift of tongues.'

'Then if the rest of your plans are in as good a state of preparation, we are indeed ready,' said the Munshi.

'When is it to be then?' asked Mrs Turnbull, a trace of cockney now returned to her voice.

And Jasper stepping forward to her said, 'The Professor told me just before he left this morning that if you passed all the Munshi's tests, my dear, we would be ready to move on time in two days.'

If Mrs Turnbull was having quite a successful morning, young Sherlock was not. He was having a very bad one. For a start he'd received the most frightful wigging for not arriving home till three o'clock in the morning. Aunt Rachel had actually waited up for him. She claimed it was the first time in her entire life that she had ever been up at such an ungodly hour. Matters had been made worse when, shortly after breakfast, the postman had brought him a package from London containing a magnifying lens which he had ordered, unbeknown to anybody, from Pillischer's in New Bond Street. It had cost him the princely sum of two pounds. The money, two golden sovereigns, had been sent him from Paris by his grandmother via Charlotte Whitney, and this of itself had caused a deal of nastiness.

'Are we then not to be trusted?' Aunt Rachel had

wailed, deeply insulted. And Gideon, round for breakfast that day, had been furious that the money had not been donated to the family coffers.

'Not that we are interested in money,' he'd boomed. 'The last thing we look for is money. But I do think you could have offered.'

The whole thing had ended with Aunt Rachel in tears and Gideon ordering him out.

'Best take your magnifying lens to your room, boy. That symbol of prodigality will only upset her the more.'

Confused and bewildered and feeling that perhaps he should have offered some part of the money towards his keep, Sherlock had retired upstairs.

He had passed the remainder of that wretched morning alone in his room. Despite the trouble it had caused him, he was immensely proud of his beautiful new magnifying lens, and he had amused himself by carrying out a minute examination of every part of the room and everything in it. Now, finally, he had come to the dressing-table and the objects thereon. Among these there happened to be that unusually large rose-thorn that he'd discovered on the floor of the woodman's hut where Natty Dan had died. Viewing it now through the glass, he noticed that there were two tiny snicks in it, one on either side. He peered at these, puzzled for some little time and then, putting down his glass, got up and ran downstairs and out into the front garden. The garden was full of rose bushes, some of them very old. He examined in turn several of the oldest, taking from each bush one or two of the largest thorns. With these he then returned to his room. Each thorn was duly examined under the glass. But none of them bore marks such as he had discovered on the thorn from the hut. He thus determined upon a little experiment.

Taking out his pocket-watch he propped it against the mirror on his dressing-table. He then placed his left hand, palm downwards, on the top of the dressing-table. With his other hand he took up the thorn from the hut floor, raised it, and with a sharp movement brought it down, jabbing its point into the back of his left hand. He then leaned back in his chair, his eyes riveted on the watch.

It was almost half-an-hour later that Mrs Cunliffe raised the alarm. Entering his room to tell him lunch was ready, she found him slumped forward over the dressing-table, breathing heavily and apparently unconscious. She immediately rushed for Aunt Rachel. By the time the Aunt got to him Sherlock was already coming round. 'Are you alright?' she asked. 'How long have you been like this?'

Sherlock glancing at his watch, said 'Twenty-two minutes and fifteen seconds precisely! It is just as I suspected!'

Without another word he leapt up and rushing past the two women, disappeared from the room.

'Sherlock! Your lunch is ready!' shouted the Aunt after him.

But he, taking the stairs two at a time, shouted back, 'Start without me! I may be some time!'

'Well, really!' said Aunt Rachel. 'That boy would try the patience of a saint!'

Sherlock hammered on the door of the doctors' house as if his life depended upon his gaining immediate admittance. When, a minute or two later, Charlotte Whitney opened the door to him, he yelled a cursory 'Hello!' and shot past her into the surgery. But there was no one there.

78

'It *is* lunchtime,' said Charlotte from the door. 'We're in the dining-room.'

'Ah! Right!' said Sherlock, and he ran along the hallway and burst in upon the doctors without hesitation or apology. 'John, is there any known poison that would give symptoms similar to those of tetanus?'

'Well, yes,' said John Whitney. 'But can't this wait?'

'No, I'm afraid it can't,' said Sherlock.

'Very well, then; some of the vegetable alkaloids, possibly,' said Whitney, who'd almost finished his lunch as it happened. 'Strychnine and the like.'

'*Strychnos nux-vomica* is a tree native to India and Ceylon from the fruit of which may be extracted strychnine,' quoted old George Sowerbutts, recalling a sentence from some text-book of long ago.

'Then is it not possible that Natty Dan might have died, not as you thought, from tetanus, but from poisoning by some such vegetable alkaloid, some strychnine-like substance?' asked Sherlock eagerly.

'I suppose that *is* possible,' admitted Whitney. 'It is also highly unlikely.'

'How do you imagine such a poison might have been administered, young'un?' asked Sowerbutts holding his plate out to Charlotte for a second helping of apple dumpling.

'I think you will find, if you carry out the appropriate tests, that this rose-thorn contains traces of such a poison,' said Sherlock, and he handed the rose-thorn from the hut floor to John Whitney.

'Ah-ha!' said old Sowerbutts. 'Someone taking a leaf from the book of the Amazonian Indians, eh? They poison their arrows with curare, you know – also a vegetable alkaloid derived from trees of the genus *strychnos* – and they propel them into the skins of their victims through a blow-pipe.' And he spooned the last drop of custard into his mouth.

'So you think that Natty Dan died because someone shot him with a poisoned arrow, do you?' said Whitney to Sherlock with a barely suppressed smile.

'Of course not!' said Sherlock tetchily.

'Then how?'

'A dog with a thorn on its paw.'

'What?' John Whitney could hardly believe his ears. Sowerbutts and Charlotte looked at each other and shrugged.

'It is entirely consistent with all the known facts,' insisted Sherlock. 'I told you I had found the tracks of a three-legged dog outside the hut, and that such a dog was almost certainly being concealed somewhere about the Manor House.'

'I have never heard such nonsense in my life!' exploded John Whitney. 'If the dog had a poisoned thorn in its paw, the poison would have killed the dog.'

'I said *on* it's paw, not *in* it,' said Sherlock smugly. 'Just suppose the thorn were the other way up?'

Then insetting one of the garden rose-thorns between the first and second fingers of his outstretched hand, he held that hand palm downwards, the thorn pointing to the floor.

Whitney was beginning to lose patience. 'In that case,' he said, 'the thorn would not be projecting into the dog's paw and the dog would have no reason to walk three-legged.'

'Ah! But might it not have been trained especially to do so, in order to prevent the thorn it was carrying from becoming blunted?' suggested Sherlock.

'Why on earth should anyone go to such lengths to kill someone like Natty Dan?' asked Charlotte.

80

'I don't think they did,' Sherlock continued. 'I think the killing of Natty Dan was pure accident. They were, if you like, experimenting on him. Well, John, will you or will you not test that thorn for poison?'

'Oh very well, then,' said John Whitney. 'Come on!' And he led the way back to the surgery.

Charlotte, it transpired, was going with her uncle on what she termed her weekly 'sick visits', so the two young men were soon alone. Long after Charlotte and Sowerbutts had gone, and while John Whitney toiled away at his work-bench, Sherlock sat in the surgery impatiently waiting the results of Whitney's test. Then, after some little time, a very serious John Whitney looked up from his work and said: 'You're right. Poison. A vegetable alkaloid, but one with which I am totally unfamiliar. How on earth did you come to suspect the rose-thorn?'

'I didn't,' admitted Sherlock, 'for some time. Then I noticed those small marks on it which indicated to me that it had been held in some metal instrument. I then asked myself why it might have been.'

'You do realise that I shall now have to notify Sergeant Grimshaw?' said Whitney. 'Natty Dan's body will have to be exhumed.'

'Just give me a few hours,' begged Sherlock. 'It is imperative that we take a closer look at the Manor House. And that we do so without further delay.'

'We?' queried John Whitney. '*We*?'

'Are you game?'

'Well . . .' John Whitney wasn't really.

'Then I shall go alone,' said Sherlock turning towards the door.

'No, wait,' said Whitney. 'I'd best come, I suppose. If only to keep you out of mischief.'

81

'That's the spirit!' said Sherlock joyously. 'The flame of adventure may be guttering and low, but at least it is not totally extinguished!' And then he noticed that John Whitney had sat himself down at his desk. 'What are you doing?' he asked.

'I must leave a note for Charlotte,' explained John. 'She'll want to know where I am.'

'Well, really!' said Sherlock. Such a thought would never have crossed his mind.

Dusk was already beginning to fall when Sherlock and John Whitney finally broke cover from Pendargh Woods and stepped onto Manor House lands, Sherlock lighting their way with an old dark-lantern belonging to Doctor Sowerbutts. There appeared to be no sign of life either at the House or in the grounds. Crouching, the pair of them ran for the shelter of the Coach House, which was the building nearest to them. Peering in at one of the windows, and perceiving the coast to be clear, Sherlock pulled one of the doors open a crack and the two of them slipped inside, pulling the door to behind them.

Sherlock made straight for the Colonel's carriage. John Whitney, meanwhile, wandered about peering into the gloom without knowing what he was supposed to be looking for. Turning back to the carriage after a while, he was unable to see Sherlock anywhere abouts. 'Sherlock!' he called. There was no sound. He opened one of the carriage doors and peered inside. It was empty. He walked all round it. There was no sign of Sherlock. He even peered under it. Nothing. He was about to leave the Coach House when Sherlock's head suddenly popped from the carriage window. 'Looking for me?' he said. John Whitney hated these tricks.

'Where were you?' he said coldly.

'I have not moved out of the carriage,' replied Sherlock.

'You see, as I suspected, it has a false bottom, a fact immediately confirmed to me by the sight of certain considerable alterations that have been made since I rode in it that day.'

'But why a false bottom?' asked Whitney. 'Smuggling?'

'In a manner of speaking, yes,' said Sherlock. 'Come on.'

As they emerged into the open again, Sherlock glanced up at the front of the house. 'John!' he said urgently. 'Look! Up there. At that window. The one with the bars over it.'

John Whitney looked. The window was only dimly lit, but the light was sufficient to reveal a woman with greying hair behind the bars. She walked with a stick, and was pacing up and down the room across the window, and apparently talking to herself.

'Who is she?' asked John Whitney.

'We are about to find out,' said Sherlock. 'I think it imperative that we get inside that house before it is too late.'

'But how?'

'Remember I used to live there. The Holmeses were ardent Royalists when this area was almost solidly Parliamentarian. They naturally took the precaution of providing bolt-holes. So, there is more than one way of getting out – and thus, more than one way of getting in. Follow me!' and he led off again, this time at a trot, back towards the woods. Some little way inside, tearing away bracken and undergrowth, he uncovered the entrance to the tunnel. 'Come on,' he said. 'In here!'

As the two of them entered, they had no idea that they were being watched.

8

The Woman in Black

The tunnel ran right under the Manor House lawns and into the house itself. Here, it diverged into a maze of tunnels, passages and concealed corridors linked by steps or short flights of stone stairs and covering practically every part of the house. Or so it had been in the time of the Civil War. Over the years, however, the warren had considerably contracted. Time had taken its toll, so too had the various alterations and 'improvements' carried out on the house down the centuries. But there was still a handy enough artery of access.

Carrying the dark-lantern Sherlock now strode out ahead, John Whitney stumbling on the uneven ground at some few paces behind him. After a while, Sherlock stopped.

'How much further?' asked the young doctor, drops of moisture from the tunnel roof dripping down his forehead and his hands already grazed from scrapes with the rough-hewn walls.

'Not far,' said Sherlock. 'We're directly beneath the stables now.'

'How do you know that?' asked Whitney.

'Ssh!' said Sherlock. 'Listen! You can hear the horses above.'

Both of them stood listening. For a time John Whitney could hear nothing but the sound of dripping and his own breathing. But then, faintly, from somewhere far above, there came the sound of whinnying and the gentle thud of hooves pawing the ground.

'My God! You've got sharp hearing,' he said to Sherlock.

Sherlock smiled and nodded. 'Now, if I remember right,' he said, 'it's a hundred and ten paces from here to the point where the tunnel enters the house. And it's uphill all the way. Come on!'

He strode off again, leaving Whitney stumbling along behind, counting: 'One, two, three, four, five . . .' Then a minute-and-a-half later: 'One-hundred-and-five, one hundred-and-six, one-hundred-and-seven, one-hundred-and-eight, one-hundred-and-nine, one-hundred-and-ten!'

By this time, Sherlock was some way ahead. All John Whitney could see was the faint glow from his lantern. 'We're in now, are we?' he said in a loud whisper.

'I've been in some time,' Sherlock called back. 'I thought you were never coming.'

The tunnel had now levelled off and opened out into a passage-way. The walls were smoother, part brick, part stone, and some sections actually wood-panelled. It was at one of the wood-panelled sections that Sherlock was standing as John Whitney came up.

'It's this panel here,' he said, pointing. 'It opens, and will bring us out, I think, into the library.' He turned a large carved wooden knob on the wall to his left.

Very slowly and silently a section of the tunnel wall began to slide open, but as it did so it revealed, no more than a foot or two in front of them, a blazing log fire and the trousered legs of Colonel Turnbull who stood before it with his back to them.

'Uh-uh!' said Sherlock, barely audibly. 'Wrong room!' John Whitney froze, terrified.

It was then that they heard Jasper's voice: 'Let me remind you, *Captain* Turnbull, that had it not been for my brother Sebastian, you would even now be rotting in a Madras jail. And don't you forget it!'

'I'm hardly likely to, am I?' replied the Colonel. 'Damned fine feller, your brother. He's the only reason I put up with you, you cocky little rasper.'

Then, after a slight pause, during which Sherlock re-activated the mechanism of the sliding panel, he added: 'Strange to think that by this time next week I shall be shot of the lot of you. Rich and single again!'

Without turning he threw the butt of his cigar into the fire. It fell at the feet of John Whitney, just a second or two before the panel slid shut.

'Phew! That was close!' said Whitney, as it shut.

'Nonsense,' said Sherlock, bending to pick up the cigar butt. 'It missed you by miles.' And he sniffed it and peered closely at it. 'Hm,' he said. 'A trichi.'

'A what?' asked John Whitney.

'A trichinopoly cigar, John. The tobacco grows near a city of that name on the Cauvery River in the Madras Presidency of Southern India. It burns to a very distinctive black ash. Now, I suggest we retrace our steps and make for the upper levels. Come on!'

He strolled off as casually as if they were promenading the park on a Sunday.

'You see, John,' he said as they went, 'there was a time when my father indulged an eccentric and expensive desire to sample the cigars of the entire world. He sold the Four Acre Field, as a matter of fact, to pay for it. It was one long, wet summer when we all seemed to have less than usual to do. And *I* devoted myself to a study of the different types of ash with which the house was soon liberally sprinkled. It is a fascinating subject. I fully intend to pursue it one day. I may even write a paper.' Suddenly he stopped dead, and putting his eye to a tiny hole in the wall said: 'Ah! This is where we get out.'

They stepped out into an empty corridor on the third floor of the Manor House. Sherlock crossed quickly to a door opposite and put his ear to it. 'Here is your barred room, John,' he said quietly.

'Are you sure?' asked Whitney nervously.

'Absolutely positive. It was formerly my nursery, hence the bars and the spy-hole opposite. Through that I could observe the panic of my Nanny when she found me missing, hiding.'

'Shall I put a shoulder to it?' said Whitney manfully, indicating the closed door.

'For what precise reason, John?' asked Sherlock.

'To get in, of course.'

'Oh I hardly think brute force will be necessary,' smiled Sherlock, and he turned the door handle and threw the door open. 'There. After you.'

It was a small, bare room with nothing in it but a dressing-table and a chair. Sherlock made straight for the dressing-table. On it stood a theatrical make-up box, and a wig block with a greying wig on it. Over the back of the chair was draped a black shawl, and propped beside it a silver-handled black ebony walking-stick.

'Well, what have they done with the prisoner?' asked Whitney, glancing round the room.

'Prisoner?' said Sherlock.

'I thought we came to rescue someone. The woman we saw from outside. The real Mrs Turnbull?'

'The *real* Mrs Turnbull?' Sherlock was at his most aggravating, and John Whitney was being aggravated.

'Sherlock, if the woman we know as Mrs Turnbull is really Bessie Bright, a music-hall impersonator, it surely follows that the person she is impersonating is the real Mrs Turnbull, and that the real Mrs Turnbull is being held somewhere here against her will.'

'I admit that thought had crossed my mind,' said Sherlock. 'Some little time ago, as a matter of fact. But it is really rather shallow reasoning, you know.'

John Whitney was getting angry. 'Then what are we doing in this house?' he asked sharply.

'Looking around. That's all,' said Sherlock.

'You realise, I suppose, that we are trespassing?'

'Oh yes,' said Sherlock, making for the door again. 'Come on!'

John Whitney, terrified of being caught on his own, was left with no option but to follow. As he came out of the nursery room he saw Sherlock entering another room a short way down the corridor on the other side. He followed him in, closing the door behind him.

This room was painted entirely in white. It was bare of furniture or pictures. There was one window with shutters. The shutters were open revealing a view out over the back of the gardens. On one wall was a calendar. On another a clock. That was all.

'Well, there's nothing in here,' said Whitney, turning back toward the door.

'On the contrary,' said Sherlock. 'I think this will tell us a good deal of what we want to know.'

'How?' said John Whitney, completely baffled.

'Look at the calendar. The date.'

John Whitney looked at it. Friday 24 November 1871. 'It's wrong,' he said.

'Yes,' replied Sherlock. 'But calendars are usually wrong because someone has forgotten to change them.

That one is already showing tomorrow's date. A very curious mistake to make. And look at the clock. What do you notice about that?'

'That's wrong, too,' said John Whitney. The hands stood at seven minutes past one. 'Or it's stopped.'

'I think not,' said Sherlock, and he took out his pocket watch and held it in his hand, glancing from watch to clock at intervals. 'One other thing,' he said eventually.

'What's that?'

'Listen,' said Sherlock.

John Whitney listened. 'I hear nothing.'

'Just so.' Sherlock's egoism was having a field-day.

'It is exactly five o'clock, yet you hear nothing. What has become of all the chiming clocks? We know there is one above the stables. It chimed the other evening as that horseman arrived. And you may have noticed when we so nearly pitched out of the fireplace into the room below that there was a grandfather clock there. From here we should certainly be able to hear it chime. But we have not. It is my opinion, John, that someone is deliberately tampering with date and time. Tomorrow this room will, I suspect, receive a visitor who will be kept here for some days. But, for reasons which I fancy we are about to discover, they are to be made to believe that they have been here no more than an hour or two.'

John Whitney was incredulous. '*What*?'

Sherlock took one more look at the clock, and glanced at his watch again before finally returning it to his pocket. 'That clock,' he then said, 'is running at precisely one twenty-fourth of its correct speed. So slowly that even the second hand appears to have stopped. Thus, in this room every twenty-four hours is being made to seem but one.'

'So there *is* to be a captive?' said John Whitney.

'Oh yes,' said Sherlock. 'Though they're not be aware that they are such. And now we know that the trap is to be sprung tomorrow. The game is afoot, John!' And he bounded to the door, opened it, peered out, then quickly shut it again, flattening himself behind. 'Ssh!' he said. 'There's someone coming!'

They heard the footsteps approach down the uncarpeted corridor. Then, from somewhere below, they heard Colonel Turnbull's voice. 'Jasper!' he shouted. From the other side of the door, Jasper replied, 'Yes?'

'Albert Bates is here.'

'Alright. I'll come straight down.'

The footsteps retreated back down the corridor.

Sherlock and John Whitney now carefully worked their way down to the second floor, peering into each room they passed. All the rooms were quite empty, devoid even of furniture. They were making their way down the stairs to the first floor when, peering over the bannister rail, they saw below them two Indian servants. Each of them carried a fully-dressed tailor's dummy.

'I suspect we want to be where they are going,' said Sherlock. And they crept down the remainder of the stairs and set off following.

The two Indians walked to the end of the corridor where there was a T-junction, and then turned off to their right and disappeared from view.

Sherlock and Whitney were about to follow round the corner when, from their left, they heard voices approaching. They flattened themselves against the wall. Shortly, Colonel Turnbull and Jasper, deep in conversation, passed along the corridor in the direction taken by the two Indians. A few paces behind them wandered a third man, a man Sherlock had not seen before. He was young, tall, well-built, fair-haired, with a pleasant open face. 'An outdoor man,' noted Sherlock, as the man passed slowly along the corridor behind the others, looking with great interest at the pictures that lined the walls.

Sherlock allowed him to get a few yards past them and then, signalling John Whitney to follow him, stepped out and took the right turn. As he did so a large black retriever dog bounded down the corridor behind them and leapt at Sherlock, almost knocking him to the floor. Whitney, panic-stricken, bolted back round the corner. But Sherlock, recovering quickly, bent and began patting the animal. 'Ssh! Ssh! There's a good fellow!' The dog began to lick his face, its tail wagging furiously.

Sherlock took one of its front paws in his hand and examined it. He beckoned Whitney out of hiding. 'Here, John, is your missing black retriever. This right front paw shows clear signs of how the poisoned rose-thorn is attached.'

Then from around the next corner up ahead they heard the voice, a rich Lancastrian voice, calling: 'Hey! Where are you? Where've you got to, eh?' The tall, fair-haired outdoor man came into view.

John Whitney again beetled for cover. Sherlock, looking up, said conversationally: 'It's alright. I've got him.'

'Oh ta!' said the Lancastrian.

'Go to your Master!'

And the dog bounded to the stranger.

'He's a beauty, isn't he?' said Sherlock.

'Aye,' said the other. 'But he's mischievous. Come on, Clinker. There's a lovely dog. Well, s'long for now, then,' and raising the first and second fingers of his right hand to his forehead, by way of salute, he wandered back away down the corridor, the dog loping at his heels.

'Bye,' shouted Sherlock after him.

'God, that was quick-thinking!' said Whitney, re-emerging. 'But what if the dog hadn't been his?'

'Ah, but he so obviously was, John. There is a certain unmistakable look that comes into a dog's eyes when it hears its master's voice.'

'He didn't even ask who you were.'

'Why should he have done? I behaved as if I belonged here. And for all he knows I do. He is quite obviously a stranger to the house himself. Did you not notice the interest he showed in the pictures?'

'So the dog belongs to him, and not to Colonel Turnbull,' said Whitney.

'Precisely!' replied Sherlock. 'It has been here these past few weeks for training, no doubt.'

It was some little time later that, opening a door on the ground floor, Sherlock found what he was looking for. 'Ah! Our friends the dummies!' he said. 'This I suspect is the centre of operations.' They slipped inside.

It was an unusually large room. Running along one side was a long, low, raised wooden platform, with a short flight of steps up at either end. About halfway along this platform stood a door frame. It was supported by wooden braces and anchored by large weights. Close to it stood a small round table and a low button-backed velvet covered arm-chair. Grouped

92

between the door-frame and the table stood the four outfitters dummies. There were two male figures and two female. All of them were formally dressed, and one wore Indian clothes and a turban. Marked out on the floor parallel to the wooden platform were a number of white lines.

'Clearly an architectural plan,' said Sherlock immediately. 'Every symbol is correct and almost certainly to scale.'

'It's a strangely shaped building,' said John Whitney. 'So long and narrow.'

But by now, Sherlock had crossed the room to the opposite wall, along which were ranged a number of wooden benches and chairs. There was also a table. It was littered with odds and ends, pencils, sheets of paper, sticks of chalk, paint pots and brushes, and various oddments and off-cuts of cloth, leather, wood and card. Sherlock rooted through the junk eagerly, finally lifting a sheet of white card and uncovering a black wooden box about the size of a small tea-caddy. He opened it and held it up triumphantly for John Whitney to see. 'This, John, is what I've been looking for ever since we entered this house!'

'What is it?' said John, crossing to him.

'It is the instrument that killed Natty Dan!' With a flourish Sherlock took from the box a ring of black elastic similar to that which Sergeant Grimshaw had used to tie round his mushrooms. The only difference was that this one held a large rose-thorn set into the leather pad and firmly secured by a square of leather glued across its back. 'You can see how snugly and inconspicuously this simple but potentially deadly device would slip onto Clinker's paw,' he said. 'The dog's hair would completely conceal it.' Suddenly he stopped, listening hard. 'I think I can hear footsteps,' he said after a moment or two. 'They are some way off, but they are coming this way.'

'I'll look,' said John Whitney, making for the door. Some seconds later he whispered: 'There's a mob of them coming!'

Sherlock glanced quickly round the room. At the far end, opposite the door, was a pile of old packing cases. tea chests, boxes, planks, baulks of timber and suchlike. 'Quick!' he said. 'Behind that lumber in the corner!' The two of them dived behind the pile as the Colonel, Jasper, Ranjeet, several Indian servants, and the fair-haired open-air man entered. The latter was now dressed in the uniform of a railwayman, and his dog carried strapped round its neck a collecting box bearing the words 'Please help the Widows and Orphans.'

'*I* know!' whispered John Whitney to Sherlock. 'The plan drawn on the floor. It's a railway station!'

'Exactly!' replied Sherlock.

'You mean you knew?'

'Oh yes. There are several pointers,' said Sherlock, at the same time keeping a close watch on what was happening in front of them. 'The manner in which that man with the dog touched his forehead to me as he left, for example. It is a form of salutation prevalent, I have observed, among men who wear peaked caps.'

'But the peaked cap is not unique to railwaymen,' objected Whitney as forcibly as he dared in the circumstances.

'Agreed,' said Sherlock. 'But look at his stance. It is entirely indicative of a man who spends a good deal of his time leaning on a luggage trolley. A railway porter, I would submit. And we already know that the Station

Master from Preston has been a regular visitor to this house.'

By this time, Ranjeet had seated himself at the rickety table. Jasper was perched on one of the wooden benches. The Colonel and the railway porter stood together at one end of the wooden platform.

'Now,' said Ranjeet to the Colonel, 'I want you to go right through it from the beginning. This is the last time we shall any of us hear it.'

'Very well,' said the Colonel. 'If we are all ready . . .' Then, looking round the room: 'Where the devil's that ruddy woman got to now?'

From outside a woman's voice said imperiously: 'We are here, Colonel Turnbull!'

The door opened, and there entered a short, dumpy, woman of about fifty with greying hair. She was dressed entirely in black, and she walked with a stick.

'My God!' whispered John Whitney. 'The Queen!'

Sherlock looked at him and smiled. 'Yes,' he said. 'Victoria Regina. According to *The Era* Bessie Bright used to set the Old Mo alight with that one. And I have to admit she is certainly very good.'

9

The Glass Cutter's Hand

Mrs Turnbull, clearly glorying in her role as Queen Victoria, moved graciously towards the velvet chair on the wooden platform, acknowledging everybody in turn with a regal inclination of her head. She took her time, and it was obvious that Colonel Turnbull felt she was over-doing it. As she finally settled herself in the chair, he glared at her and snorted. She, smiling warmly, said in the unmistakable tones of the Queen: 'We are ready when you are, Colonel.' And he snorted again.

'Right then,' he began. 'This,' indicating the area enclosed by white lines on the floor, 'is the platform at Lancaster Station. It is Friday 24 November. At one o'clock the Royal Train en route from Ballater, near Balmoral, to Windsor, will stop here in order that luncheon may be carried aboard. During this brief break in her journey Her Majesty has graciously consented to make a contribution to the public subscription presently being raised on behalf of the Distressed Widows and Orphans of Railwaymen. Now, Bates here, the Station's Senior Porter, has devised the wholly original idea of using a dog for the purpose of soliciting contributions. And Her Majesty, whose fondness for the canine race is legendary, has expressed a desire to meet Clinker in person. The dog's recent absence from its usual place at the station has, incidentally, been attributed to its having suffered a slight accident to its paw.'

'I told 'em as 'e'd sprained 'is foot rabbitting,' put in

the Lancastrian. 'He did once an' all. Daft ha'p'orth!'

'Quite so,' said Colonel Turnbull, glaring. 'So, the Royal Train is now at the platform, Bates. When Her Majesty is ready, you will be summoned into the Royal presence. You will by now, of course, have "prepared" the dog in the manner prescribed. You know exactly when and where?'

'Aye,' said the porter with complete self-assurance.

'And you know the signals?'

'Aye,' said Bates again. And he gave a low staccato whistle, a single short blast. The dog immediately raised its right front paw from the ground. Bates whistled again, two short blasts this time. The dog put its paw down again.

'Good,' said the Colonel. 'Sounds hardly likely to be remarked upon in the din of a railway station. Now, you walk the dog towards the train.'

Bates gave a single short whistle and began walking towards the Colonel. The dog, its paw raised off the ground, walked at his side.

'You thus prevent the thorn becoming blunted,' continued the Colonel. 'But once you enter the Royal Saloon and step onto carpet, you signal the dog to walk normally.'

Bates did so, and the dog immediately obeyed.

'Now, when you are admitted to the Royal Saloon you will find several other members of the Household present, as represented by these dummies.' He introduced them in turn. 'The Munshi. He is Her Majesty's Indian private secretary. A most trusted Royal servant, and a man almost fanatically devoted to the success of our cause. There will also be a Lady-in-Waiting, probably the Marchioness of Ely; and there will almost certainly be the fourteen year old Princess

Beatrice. So, you enter the Saloon . . .'

Bates and the dog were now entering through the braced door-frame and approaching the seat on which Mrs Turnbull sat. As they reached her, Bates removed his cap, and the dog sat.

'Right,' continued the Colonel. 'Now, Her Majesty will no doubt have a brief word with you. She will then drop a few coins (sovereigns almost certainly) into the collecting box.' And turning suddenly on Mrs Turnbull, he barked: 'Right you – the coins!' There was something about her easy assumption of the regal manner that irritated him.

Mrs Turnbull took a few coins from the small leather purse she carried, and dropped them one by one with premeditated slowness into the box that hung from the dog's neck. Immediately, the dog lifted its front right paw and slapped it down on her thigh in a 'Thank you' gesture, wagging its tail like mad.

John Whitney was absolutely horrified. 'So, it's a plot to assassinate the Queen!' he hissed at Sherlock.

'I think you will find it is a good deal more devious than that,' replied Sherlock. 'Remember the White Room.'

Meanwhile, in front of them, the proceedings had been halted by Albert Bates, whose simple practical mind had perceived a couple of possible flaws in the Professor's great scheme.

''Ere, I say,' he said to the Colonel. 'Won't she yell when t'thorn jabs 'er?'

'Mr Bates,' said Mrs Turnbull at her most regal. 'We are well trained to suffer such trifling irritations in silence, and not to remark on the over-long nails of our subjects' pet dogs!'

Jasper stifled a laugh. He was full of admiration

98

for Bessie in this role. But Ranjeet and the Colonel were impatient at the interruption. However, Bates was not to be put off. Turning to the Colonel once more he said, in a deeply confidential tone, 'Any road, that little thorn might not go through all Her Majesty's er . . . you know . . . er . . .' And he whispered the word 'under-garments.' 'They do say she wears more underneath than most of us wear on top,' he added knowingly.

Jasper burst out laughing. But Ranjeet glared at him and he soon stopped. 'Can we just show him how effective that thorn is?' he said, and he signalled to one of the Indian servants, who was standing off the end of the wooden platform beside the fifth of the tradesmen's dummies. The Indian lifted the dummy's skirt to reveal the thigh section beneath. It was covered with a wafer-thin cushion simulating flesh. This had been ripped to pieces.

'Jumpin' Jehoshaphat!' exclaimed Bates. 'It'll not kill 'er, will it? I'd not want no part of that, 'undred quid or no!'

'Mr Bates,' said Ranjeet very firmly, quashing any desire on the part of anyone to laugh, 'that dummy has been used many, many times in practice. In reality there will be one tiny puncture. We have experimented over many months now. Precisely the correct dosage will be given. We have even tested it on a human being. We know precisely when she will pass out and for how long. Her Majesty will begin to be affected half way between Lancaster and Preston. Halfway!'

'And there,' whispered Sherlock to John Whitney, 'is the reason that Natty Dan was chosen. He had the misfortune, you see, to be the same build as the Queen, and thus ideal for their experiments.'

99

'But he died!' exclaimed John Whitney.

'Obviously that over-friendly dog, unbeknown to them, followed him to the hut that night and gave him an extra, unplanned, and fatal dose of the drug,' Sherlock explained.

By this time, Albert Bates' part in the affair was done. Leading Clinker from the platform, he walked to the back of the room, not many paces from where John Whitney and Sherlock were hidden. Suddenly, the dog picked up the scent of the two men behind the crates. Wagging his tail furiously, he began pawing at them.

'Go away!' hissed Sherlock.

But the dog just gave a friendly yelp, and Albert Bates, bending to see what was attracting it, came face to face with Sherlock.

'Oh! 'Ello! It's you!' he said, assuming that Sherlock was playing some important, but as yet unrevealed role in the plot. ''Ow are yer?'

Jasper's attention had already been drawn. Rising and signalling the others to follow, he moved towards the hiding place.

'I say, old chap,' said Sherlock to Bates, 'do you mind stepping aside? This is a most tricky part of the operation and we must have room.'

'Sorry!' said Bates. And giving his little salute, he vanished from Sherlock's view.

'Now,' said Sherlock to John Whitney. 'When I say go, push and go!' And a second or two later he yelled, 'GO!' and the two of them pushed with all their strength against the crates in front of them and, leaping over anything in their way, rushed for the door.

'After them,' shouted Jasper, leading the others in chase.

As they all vanished, shouting, from the room,

Albert Bates turned to Mrs Turnbull and said: 'Well, it all seems to be going very smoothly, don't it?'

Mrs Turnbull glared at him. 'Fool!' she snapped.

Sherlock moved fast along the corridors of the Manor House, with John Whitney close behind. 'We'll make for the Drawing Room,' he shouted over his shoulder. 'The panel behind the fireplace, and out the way we came!'

They sped across the entrance hall into the room, John Whitney slamming the door behind him and turning the key in the lock. Sherlock, meanwhile, at the fireplace, reached for the carved wooden rosette that operated the panel mechanism from inside the room. But as he turned it, it crumbled into several pieces and came away in his hand. 'Wood-worm!' he muttered. 'There's no escape this way!' He made his way back to the door, unlocked it and peered out into the hall. It was silent and deserted.

'Look!' said John Whitney. 'The front door's open! They must think we went that way. Let's go!'

But Sherlock grabbed his arm. 'No!' he said. 'It could be a trap. They're probably waiting for us out there. We'll make for the upstairs entrance to the secret passage,' and he led John Whitney out into the entrance hall. They had got about half way across when, from above, there was a faint swishing sound and a large net dropped over them, tumbling them over onto the floor in a helpless heap. From the shadowy recesses there now stepped Jasper, Ranjeet and Colonel Turnbull. The Colonel had a hypodermic syringe in his hand.

'Right, Colonel, if you're ready with the injections,' said Jasper. And they advanced on the figures struggling in the net.

Sherlock's drugged sleep was deep, dream-filled and fantastic, and it was with some regret that he eventually found himself returning to the realities of the world, knowing neither where he was, nor for how long he had been away.

He awoke to find himself lying in bed. He was wearing a night-shirt. His head throbbed and the bare walls and ceiling of the room seemed to undulate and sway as he looked at them. He tried to focus his eyes on a lamp that hung from the ceiling, but it kept advancing and receding until he could look at it no longer. Then, distantly, echoing, he heard a voice.

'Ah! So you're coming back to us at last are you, young feller? Good for you!'

Sherlock raised his head ever so slightly off the pillow. The effort was enormous. It felt so heavy. But before he slumped back again he just managed to make out a tall, dark, bearded man standing at the foot of the bed.

'Where am I?' he murmured, lying quite still, his eyes barely open.

'In hospital,' said the man. 'The Royal Infirmary, Preston. I'm Doctor Greasley. You and your companion there,' and he indicated John Whitney who lay in a bed a few feet away, still dead to the world, 'were found unconscious in Avenham Park one evening last week.'

'Last week?' said Sherlock, hazily. 'What day is this, then?'

'It's Friday,' said the doctor.

Friday! Sherlock saw again in his mind's eye the calendar on the wall of the White Room at the Manor House. 'Friday 24 November!' he said aloud.

'No,' said the Doctor. 'Friday 1 December.'

What? Had a whole week passed? Had they been

there all that time? He could remember nothing after the net and the syringe.

'Then we are too late,' he said, and he closed his eyes. A black despair engulfed him. Then he heard the doctor's voice again:

'Too late for what?'

Summoning all his strength and concentration, Sherlock raised himself onto one elbow. 'We overheard a plot to abduct the Queen,' he said. And as he outlined what he knew of affairs at the Manor House, John Whitney too came back to consciousness.

'We tried to prevent it,' John murmured weakly.

'Oh I don't expect you to believe us,' concluded Sherlock.

But the doctor did believe him.

'That whole affair has been extensively reported by the newspapers,' he said. 'Don't worry. It didn't happen. Some railway porter got the wind up and gave the game away.'

'Bates!' muttered Sherlock.

'Yes, I think that was the name,' said the doctor and he drew a folded newspaper from his coat pocket.

'There's more,' he said, 'in this morning's *Preston Guardian*. ''Plot to kidnap Queen foiled by local railway porter.'' Then there's a long and detailed account. So there we are,' he said, folding the newspaper and returning it to his pocket. 'It's all over. Now, your families have been informed that you are both safe and in hospital. It will take a day or two to get you back to full health, that's all. I suggest you get some rest.'

'Thank you,' said Sherlock. 'You have lifted a considerable weight from our minds.'

Doctor Greasley left the room.

'Thank God that's all over,' said John Whitney,

settling down to sleep again.

'I don't think it is all over,' said Sherlock, and he swung himself out of bed. 'Come, John, you must pull yourself together. Sit up.'

Whitney struggled to do so. He was still very drowsy.

'Concentrate your mind, John!' barked Sherlock. 'Just consider these curious facts. One. Why should that man profess to be reading from the *Preston Guardian* whilst holding a copy of *The Western Morning News*?' John Whitney stared at him blankly. 'Well, anyone with the most elementary knowledge of newspaper typography could tell you that. Two. That man is no more a doctor than I am. The marks on his hands clearly indicate that he is a glass-cutter by trade. Three. What is that tobacco ash doing on the floor under that chair? This is supposed to be a hospital. Trichinopoly, unless my eyes deceive me.'

John Whitney tried desperately to focus his eyes on the tiny mound of black ash, but even the chair appeared as no more than a shadowy blur to him.

'Concentrate! Concentrate!' said Sherlock firmly. 'Colonel Turnbull smokes trichis, you may remember. But, unless I am much mistaken, we have even more persuasive evidence.' He pulled up his left sleeve. 'Yes! Look there!' pointing to a mark on his fore-arm. 'Had it all happened a week ago that needle puncture would have healed by now, would it not?'

'Why, yes! Of course it would!' said Whitney. He was beginning to realise the seriousness of their situation, and this was having a wonderfully clearing effect upon his mind.

Sherlock leapt from the bed and examined the wall opposite. On it he noticed two groups of small nail

104

holes. 'The White Room!' he said aloud. 'When we were last here those holes were obscured by a clock and a calendar.' He went to the window and opened the shutters. No more did they reveal a view across the back lawns. The window had been bricked up.

He then noticed a small white-painted cupboard standing against the end wall. It had not been there the last time. He opened it. Inside lay their clothes. He threw them onto one of the beds. 'Here,' he said to John Whitney. 'Dress!'

John clambered from his bed. 'You haven't yet tried the door,' he said.

'Locked and bolted,' replied Sherlock, pulling on his trousers. 'Beautifully engineered, well-oiled, and expertly turned and shot, I grant you, but it did not escape *my* ears. No, we have to wait until they return and open that door themselves. The thing is to be ready when they come.'

He reached across to the bed-side table and tipped the water carafe onto its side. The water poured out all over the floor, finally subsiding to a trickle. John Whitney, about to button his shirt, stared in amazement. Sherlock then picked up one of his own shoes and walking to the middle of the room placed it very carefully on its side, setting its position in relation to the door and the beds with great precision.

'What in Heaven's name are you doing?' asked John Whitney.

'John, when they come back, we must be in bed,' explained Sherlock. 'Now if they look in through that peep-hole . . .'

'Peep-hole?' said Whitney.

'You notice nothing, John!' said Sherlock. 'In the door. Now, if they look in and see the beds are empty, they will be suspicious. If, on the other hand, they look in and see us both lying there supine, they may very well go away again. Thus, it is imperative that we arouse their curiosity sufficiently to ensure that they open that door and enter this room. And who could resist investigating an upset water carafe and a solitary abandoned shoe?'

'And in the meantime?' asked John Whitney, who was not at all sure that his plan would succeed.

'In the meantime,' replied Sherlock, 'we lie in bed, feigning sleep, but holding ourselves in readiness to jump anyone who comes in.'

It was just as the doctor had told them. Their families *had* been notified. Though only Sherlock's had been told the hospital tale.

First news had been carried to Aunt Rachel late on the Thursday evening by Sergeant Grimshaw himself. He had arrived full of reassurance (and very cool towards Mrs Cunliffe) having, as he explained, received 'a most urgent message from the Infirmary.'

The precise words of that message had been chosen, unbeknown to him and with the greatest attention to detail, by none other than The Professor himself. It had referred to Sherlock and John Whitney having been found wandering the streets of Preston 'delirious' and had mentioned 'fever' and 'quarantine' more than once, thus arousing in Aunt Rachel's imagination the spectre of that typhoid that had brought Sherlock home early for the holiday.

Next morning Gideon had arrived for breakfast to find his sister in a state of high anxiety. Charity had seemed a little pale first thing. And tired. She had actually yawned. She had been seen to shiver as she

·dressed (it was only November, and not especially chill). Now, as they both stared at her, she looked flushed. Oh yes, she'd been sitting by the fire alright, but wasn't that flush just a little *too* bright? Her temperature had been taken every half-hour, and her pulse. Both appeared normal. But Aunt Rachel knew well enough that these were unreliable indicators.

So Charity was set in the parlour; and Mrs Cunliffe was instructed to keep the fire well banked up, and to give her whatever she felt like by way of food or drink; and she was watched by everybody throughout the day like a time-bomb ticking in their midst. She was thoroughly enjoying it.

No one thought any more of Sherlock.

It was not Sergeant Grimshaw who called on Doctor Sowerbutts and Charlotte Whitney with news of John. It was a tall, burly, sailor-man, with a deep scar across his right cheek and a gold ear-ring, and he came early on the Friday morning. He'd met the two young men he described in such detail in an ale house on Preston Quay very late the previous night, and had been offered a sovereign to deliver the cryptic message that he had committed to memory: 'The fox has broken cover and the hounds have given chase. What ever tales you may hear abroad . . .' (A clever touch that. A last-minute addition of the Professor's in case either Charlotte or Sowerbutts should bump into Aunt Rachel!). '. . . Whatever tales you may hear abroad, smile and acquiesce. Do nothing till we send word.' This message the scarred sailor delivered in a rich, ripe, salty accent redolent of years spent before the mast.

'You have brought us great relief, my man,' said old George Sowerbutts, finally. 'And have most nobly

107

earned your sovereign.'

'The gen'l'man in question give me an 'alf-sovereign, sir,' explained the tar. 'He said as I'd collect t'other 'alf on delivery, like.'

'Dear cautious, John!' smiled Charlotte, happy again after the early worry of discovering that her husband had not come home the previous night.

Old George Sowerbutts ferreted in his pocket and finally passed a half-sovereign to the messenger, at the same time making a mental note to get it back from John Whitney when next he saw him.

It was almost ten o'clock that morning when Doctor Greasley got back to the Manor House. As he entered, he was whistling the sailor's hornpipe and flicking his half-sovereign in the air.

An hour later, Jasper Moran returned. He that morning had paid a brief visit to Aunt Rachel, ostensibly to offer sympathy and every possible assistance, but in fact to ensure that the Professor's tale had been believed and that no one had any intention of doing anything foolish, such as trying to visit Sherlock. He needn't have worried. No one had the slightest intention. However, he returned bearing a set of verses which had been copied in beautiful copper-plate by Charity herself from a magazine called *The Children's Friend*. These Jasper had gleefully promised to deliver to Sherlock at the Infirmary later that day. But first things first . . .

The sound of hooves and carriage wheels approaching on the gravel of the drive now told him that the time had come to move.

All was ready. It was now forty-five minutes before the Royal train was due to arrive at Lancaster Station.

10

The Unexpected Visitors

Sherlock appeared to be sleeping like a baby when John Whitney tapped him on the shoulder to tell him that he could hear footsteps approaching down the corridor.

'Lie down, lie still,' hissed Sherlock. 'Wait till whoever it is comes right into the room. They'll go for the shoe first. As soon as they bend to pick it up, we hit them!' They both lay down again, feigning sleep. Each of them had a shoe clutched tightly in his hand.

The footsteps drew closer and stopped. An eye appeared briefly at the peep-hole. The bolts were drawn back, the key turned in the lock, and the door edged very slowly open by this cautious visitor. He entered the room stealthily, carefully stepping over the shoe, and totally ignoring the upset water carafe. He made straight for where Sherlock lay and, reaching him, bent low over him.

There was a muffled yell and Sherlock, uncoiling like a spring, was on him! At the same moment, John Whitney, shoe in hand, leapt from his bed to join the assault.

There was a terrified yell. 'It's me! It's me! Stop it! It's me!!' The attack ceased abruptly.

'Newbugs?' said Sherlock, extremely surprised. 'What are you doing here?'

'Last night. I were watching,' replied the lad, rubbing the back of his neck where John Whitney had landed his first clout, and looking rather sorry for himself. 'I seed you come in. So's I waited. And when you never come out, I come in arter you.'

Sherlock and Whitney were both quite touched, and
very apologetic. Did he know how many people were
now in the house? Oh yes. And he described them.
Jasper, Ranjeet and Greasley.

'What about the Colonel and Mrs Turnbull?' asked
Sherlock.

'Gone.'

'In the carriage?'

'Ah.'

'Time to make a move,' said Sherlock.

They made their way back to the great Drawing
Room, without encountering a soul. Here Sherlock
seated himself at the desk and scribbled a quick note
which he addressed to an old friend of his father's,
Colonel Hamilton, Commander of the garrison at
Fulwood Barracks, Preston. 'You know Doctor
Sowerbutts?' he asked Newbugs.

'Yes. The de-lousing man,' said Newbugs who
harboured bitter memories.

'Well, just one of his talents,' smiled Sherlock.
'Anyway, you're to take this to him and tell him to
ensure that it is delivered with all possible speed. Go
on! Off with you! And run like a deer!'

Newbugs raced from the room.

It was Greasley who discovered that the prisoners had
escaped from the white room.

'Jasper! Ranjeet!' he yelled. 'The room's empty!
They've gone!'

As he ran into the entrance hall, Jasper and Ranjeet
came racing down the stairs.

'They must be found!' shouted the Indian angrily.
Sherlock intended making it easy for them. 'Looking

110

for someone?' he called from the Drawing Room.

John Whitney already stood behind the door holding above his head a heavy bronze statuette that he had grabbed from the mantlepiece. Unbeknown to him it was a favourite possession of Ranjeet's, being an excellent likeness of Nana Sahib who had led the Indian Mutiny of 1857 and been responsible for one of its bloodiest episodes, the massacre of the British at Cawnpore. However, Fate intervened to prevent the irony of the Indian being felled with his own hero. It was Greasley who entered first and went down under Nana Sahib.

Ranjeet and Jasper fared little better. They fell in quick succession to Sherlock's considerable skill as a bare-knuckle pugilist. It was an art he had acquired from his father's friends many of whom, in the 1860s, had belonged to that fraternity known as 'The Corinthian Fancy' when its prize-fighting heroes were men like Tom Sayers, Jem Mace and Tom King.

'Right, come on,' urged John Whitney. 'Let's get ourselves out of here and down to the railway station.' He stepped carefully over the prostrate Greasley to replace the statuette on the mantlepiece.

'Patience, John! Patience!' said Sherlock. 'The railway station is taken care of. We must guard these birds until the military arrive.'

This suggestion was obviously not much to poor Whitney's liking. He was very nervous and not a little confused. 'One thing, Sherlock,' he asked, almost desperately. 'If this plot was not to assassinate the Queen, what on earth were they up to?'

'I should have thought that was evident by now. A false-bottomed carriage; a room where time was slowed to one twenty-fourth; a woman impersonating the

111

Queen. Obviously, she was to be substituted when the train reached Preston.'

'But how?'

'Well, we know the Queen was to be given a mild poison, aimed to ensure that she was taken ill somewhere between Lancaster and Preston. At Preston the train would be stopped so that they could telegraph ahead for medical assistance. I imagine that our Colonel, aided and abetted by the Munshi, would identify the illness as some rare and virulent disease that required immediate attention. He would place his carriage at her disposal to rush her to hospital. The Munshi would travel with her, of course. But he was part of the plot.'

'Ah, yes,' said John Whitney, 'but a Lady-in-Waiting would go with her, surely?'

'Of course. But it would take less than ten seconds to effect the substitution and I'm sure the Munshi could see to it that a Lady-in-Waiting was kept out of the carriage for that short time. Other servants might travel on the box. But they would see and hear nothing amiss. Other members of the household would, no doubt, follow close behind, and the carriage would not for a moment be out of their sight. It would make no difference. When they arrived at Preston Hospital, it would be the 'double' that went in, to emerge, quite shortly, cured, and to return to the train and thence to Windsor.'

'And the Queen herself?'

'Heavily drugged, she would be brought here and held in the white room for, I imagine, a couple of days. And should she, in her hazy state, happen to notice the clock or the calendar, she would believe herself to have been there no more than a couple of hours – the precise time her "double" had spent in Hospital.'

'And the purpose of all this?'

'Do you know,' said Sherlock, 'I'm not yet certain of that. But I fancy it has something to do with the Eye of the Peacock and this maharajah chap.' He handed Whitney a letter he'd found in a drawer of the desk.

The young doctor's eyes flicked briefly down the page. 'Dhuleep Singh,' he said, thoughtfully. 'Wasn't he that disinherited infant maharajah of the Punjab?'

'The same,' said Sherlock, his eyes gleaming. 'Now idol of London society and a favourite of the Queen's. You see from the letter that he has accepted an invitation to visit Her Majesty at Windsor the day after tomorrow.'

'And you suppose that fact to have some significance?'

'I fancy it tells us what this whole affair is about,' replied Sherlock enigmatically.

It was now 1.35 P.M. The Royal train was standing at Lancaster Station. Luncheon was over. Albert Bates and Clinker were being ushered into the Royal Saloon by the Munshi.

Except for the fact that the three men who lay unconscious on the floor were not drunk, the scene at the Manor House some forty minutes later resembled that of many a country squire's home after dinner. John Whitney sat in an arm chair reading Volume One of a leather-bound edition of Blair's *Lectures on Rhetoric*. Sherlock was stretched out in another chair opposite, his eyes closed, totally relaxed. There was a loud banging at the front door.

'That must be the military!' said Whitney with great

relief. And he got up and hurried towards the entrance hall.

'They've made good time,' muttered Sherlock. He didn't even open his eyes.

The young doctor threw open the front door expecting to see a red-coated officer and a small troop of horse. But there was not a soul in sight.

'Sherlock!' he shouted. 'There's no one here!'

'Are you sure?' said Sherlock appearing as if by magic in the hall. And he bounded to the front door and ran down the steps, scanning the grounds. 'Curious,' he murmured. And then it dawned. 'Idiot!' he shouted. 'A trick! An elementary trick!' He raced back into the great Drawing Room just in time to see the panel behind the fireplace sliding shut. Jasper, Ranjeet and Greasley had gone. And with them the statuette of Nana Sahib.

'Quick!' he yelled to John Whitney, turning back to the door again. 'Someone's opened the panel from the secret passage. Into the woods! The tunnel entrance!'

But it was already too late. There was a faint whirring sound followed by a series of loud metallic crashes. Across every window and across the door there dropped a metal shutter. Rapidly the darkness enclosed them. Sherlock lunged for the dark-lantern that stood on a side-table, and lit it.

'Ssh!' he said suddenly. He froze, listening.

From somewhere above there came a faint hissing sound. 'Unless I am much mistaken that's gas of some sort,' said Sherlock.

'Quick, the lantern!' yelled Whitney. 'Put it out! I'll see to the fire!' But as he turned towards it, the light began to die of its own volition. It was soon completely extinguished.

'Carbon dioxide!' said Sherlock, recognising its properties. 'So, they intend to asphyxiate us! It is considerably heavier than air. We must get above it. Climb on the furniture, John. As high as we can go.'

They clambered towards the ceiling, carefully picking out hand and foot holds on the shelves and ornamental carvings of the tall old-fashioned furniture.

It was now 2.30 P.M. Colonel Turnbull's carriage was standing in the station yard at Preston. Out on the platform the Colonel was discussing the lepidoptera of India with the Station Master, Mr Prendergast, when the signal on the down line changed and a distant whistle was heard.

'Ah! That'll be the Royal train,' said the Station Master, pulling out his watch and glancing at it. 'And running exactly to time.' .

Sherlock was worried. It was apparent that something had gone dreadfully wrong. The military had not arrived as they should have done. The only air left in the room was a thin layer extending two or three feet below the ceiling. John Whitney and he could go no higher and Whitney especially was beginning to show signs of exhaustion. His head was swimming, he felt dizzy, and he knew he could not hold on much longer to his precarious perch on the narrow ledge of furniture.

Rapidly, Sherlock reviewed the events leading up to their imprisonment. And then he remembered.

Just before the grilles had dropped in and the gas had started to enter, he had heard a clattering noise like an anchor chain being paid out. It had come from somewhere immediately above. So, the control

mechanism must be up there. If only he could get to it.
And there was a way. The chimneys. They inter-
connected. He remembered tales of the little climbing
boys the sweeps had at one time used, and how one had
emerged unexpectedly into his father's room while he
was shaving. So, if Sherlock climbed the chimney in
the Drawing Room, he could come down the one in the
room above.

John Whitney was sceptical. 'You'd never make it.
The gas in the chimney. Or you'd get stuck.'

'Nevertheless,' said Sherlock, 'I can try. Wish me
luck, John. And for God's sake, keep awake. If you
fall, you have no chance whatever. Count aloud; recite
the alphabet; a poem – anything . . .' And taking a
deep lungful of air, he jumped to the ground, entered
the fireplace, and began climbing. As he went, working
his way up with elbows and knees, his lungs almost
bursting, the soot and mortar showering about him and
down into the fireplace, he heard John's voice
mechanically reciting:-

> 'I remember, I remember
> The House where I was born,
> The little window where the sun
> Came peeping in at morn;
> He never came a wink too soon
> Nor brought too long a day;
> But now, I often wish the night
> Had borne my breath away . . .'

With a slither and a whoosh, amid brick and soot,
Sherlock landed in the room above. His father's
bedroom looked now like a cross between the fly-floor
of some old theatre and the deck of a man-o'-war.
Ropes hung everywhere, and there was a good deal of

116

block and tackle about. Counterweighted shafts or barrels ran across the ceiling. Around the walls was a rail like a pin rail with its cleats and ropes tied off. Drums like capstans or winches were lined at either end, and the floor was a maze of link-chain and cable.

Sherlock shouted back down the chimney. 'John! I'm up here! I'll have you out in a few minutes! John! *John*!

There was no answering shout.

'JOHN!!!' His voice echoed away to silence.

John Whitney lay motionless on the floor. Sherlock, realising what must have happened, worked quickly, assessing the purpose of each line and its mode of operation at a glance. Within a minute, the shutters over the Drawing Room door and the front door were being wound up, and Sherlock was racing down the stairs and into the room where Whitney lay. He dragged him out into the entrance hall and flung open the front door.

It was then that help arrived. It came, it seemed, from all quarters. Charlotte Whitney drove in the gig; and Captain Cholmondeley led a troop of horse up the drive. Then, from the woods, across the lawn, puffed old George Sowerbutts with Newbugs dancing ahead of him and urging him to speed. Sherlock stood at the top of the steps as they all arrived below. 'About time, too!' he said.

For Captain Cholmondeley it had been a disappointing day. On orders from his Commanding Officer, Colonel Hamilton, he had ridden at the head of a detachment of mounted troops, at full gallop, from Fulwood Barracks to Preston Station, fully expecting that he was about to thwart a plot against Her Majesty.

But he had arrived to find that the Royal train had steamed through precise to time and without mishap, and that Colonel and Mrs Turnbull whom he had been ordered to apprehend had vanished. He had then led his men back to the Manor House to apprehend Jasper Moran, Ranjeet, and Greasley. And they too had vanished. He had at one fell swoop lost his quarry, his friends, and the best subscriber to his military charity. It had been a most disappointing day.

'Unfortunately, we have no one to charge or even to interrogate,' he said miserably, as they all sat dejectedly in the library with a great feeling of anti-climax. 'We can do very little even about the Munshi without some corroborative evidence. With no one in custody . . .' He sighed, and sipped the brandy old George Sowerbutts had sympathetically handed round.

The only one who was really happy was Newbugs, and he at that moment was outside in the grounds, staring at the soldiers, an easy catch for a recruiting sergeant.

'I must say,' said Sherlock, 'that I fully expected the Turnbulls to return here to find out what had gone wrong. But we have, I suspect, seen the last of them, too.'

'One thing puzzles me,' said John Whitney who was much recovered and staring hard at Sherlock.

'What's that, John?'

'Why didn't the train stop?'

'Because, John, when I discovered that box in the Train Room, I took the elementary precaution of replacing the sharp and poisoned thorn with a perfectly harmless and blunted one. I had come prepared, you see.'

'So, the Queen was *never* in danger?' said Charlotte.

'Never,' smiled Sherlock.

'Well, you could have told me,' said John Whitney angrily. 'It would have saved me a good deal of worry.'

'I doubt it,' said Sherlock. 'You would only have found something else to worry about!'

Captain Cholmondeley, helping himself absent-mindedly to another brandy, said in confidential manner. 'Incidentally, gentlemen, it is considered advisable that no word of this matter get beyond the immediate circle of those involved.' Everybody nodded their assent.

'Of course,' said John Whitney.

'Aunt Rachel wouldn't have believed it anyway,' said Sherlock. 'She'll not hear a word against Jasper or the Turnbulls.'

For four whole days there were no further developments. Sherlock spent much of this time in his room, and the house was permeated by the sound of his violin. Uncle Gideon and Charity complained bitterly of the noise, but Aunt Rachel refused to have it stopped. 'Why that poor boy is quite obviously still suffering the effects of his illness,' she said. 'Though mercifully short and not, as I had feared, typhoid, it has clearly taken its toll. If his sad music can help him, *I* will not be the one to deny it him.'

It was about noon on the fifth day, which was a Wednesday, that Sherlock in his room heard Charity shout 'Mama! It's the Turnbulls! Colonel and Mrs Turnbull! They're coming here!'

With his violin still under his chin and his bow in his hand, he looked from his window and there stood the brown and ochre carriage. Colonel and Mrs Turnbull were just stepping out. The dirge changed to a merry jig.

The Turnbulls had arrived ostensibly to bid their adieus to the Holmeses. They were, they said, returning to India once more 'in the line of duty'. What is more they came bearing gifts. Soon Aunt Rachel was twittering over the beauty of her Kashmir shawl; Charity was squealing over the sumptuous leather-bound diary that was embossed with her name and decorated with a single red rose; Gideon was burbling with greedy delight and shovelling Indian sweetmeats into his mouth.

Amid the swelling hullabaloo, the Colonel took Sherlock to one side and handed him what appeared to be a miniature violin case.

'For you,' he said.

'Is it safe to open it?' asked Sherlock, doubtfully.

'Perfectly,' said the Colonel.

Very cautiously, Sherlock opened it. Inside, there lay a beautifully bound copy of Samuel Smiles' *Self Help* and tucked inside it a note. It read: 'You have not heard the last of the names Moran and Moriarty.' And it was signed 'Sebastian Moran.'

'So,' said Sherlock, 'it was Jasper's brother Sebastian who spirited them away! They are, I assume, on the way back to India by now?'

'We sail together this evening,' said the Colonel.

'Then be sure to thank them for the book, won't you?' said Sherlock.

Charity then sang a terrible song by way of goodbye. It was called 'The Swallows Farewell' and it was about summer going and winter coming, and ice and snow, and a lot of birds going 'over the sea in bands; to yonder far off lands.' It looked as though she'd continue for a very long time but, mercifully, the performance was terminated by the entrance of Mrs Cunliffe.

'Excuse me, Mum,' she said to Aunt Rachel, 'but were you expecting Mr Jasper? I've just seen him outside.'

The Colonel rose at once. 'Ah! It must be time to go,' he said.

Charity, eager to see Jasper again, offered to see the Colonel to his carriage. He made his good-byes and the two of them went out. Poor Mrs Turnbull was much delayed by Gideon who, with her hand held firmly in his, was burbling, 'Dear lady, dear lady, Pendargh will be a social desert without you.'

Suddenly from outside there was a flash of brilliant white light and a mighty bang. The house shook. Pictures fell from the wall. A window cracked and a sliver of plaster fell from the ceiling. There was a terrible scream.

Sherlock leapt to the window and peered out. The smoke was just clearing. 'My God,' he shouted. 'The Colonel's carriage! It's been blown up!'

Charity came screaming back into the room. Her clothes were torn, her hair was singed, her face was blackened, and she was sobbing. 'Mama! Mama!' she wailed.

Aunt Rachel, overcome by the sight of her 'baby' in such a state, took one look at her and fainted right away.

11

The Eye of the Peacock

Sherlock ran for the doctors. The Colonel was not dead. Sergeant Grimshaw, who'd heard the explosion as he was sitting with a new-found 'Cookey' in a kitchen a few doors down, arrived on the scene within minutes. He at once proclaimed a deep-dyed anarchist plot to destroy the English squirearchy. It was controlled, he said, from somewhere in Bosnia. And as anarchy was on everyone's lips in that year of 1871, those who didn't know better were quite happy to believe him.

In the kitchen, Mrs Cunliffe boiled endless water and made endless tea. Upstairs, Charity bawled (until sedated) and Aunt Rachel, recovered from her swoon, whinnied on about the wickedness of the world and how things had not been like that when she was a girl. Gideon ran up and down and in and out, managing to remain bright and cheerful but getting in everybody's way.

Mrs Turnbull sat in the front parlour for some time in a state of deep shock. She neither spoke nor moved. Eventually, still staring vacantly ahead of her, she said quietly to Captain Cholmondeley, 'Poor old codger. They didn't 'ave no need to do that to 'im, did they?' and she burst into floods of tears. The worst was over.

An hour later, completely calm, she announced her intention of turning Queen's evidence, and with Sherlock and John Whitney summoned to the room as witnesses, Captain Cholmondeley proceeded to take 'The Statement of Miss Bessie Bright'.

She told how she had been approached one night at the Music Hall by a tall, well-dressed man of about forty ('a real gentleman, he was') who had come bearing a letter of introduction from the Prime Minister.

'Moriarty!' exclaimed Sherlock.

'No! Gladstone, you fat'ead,' snapped Bessie, who knew perfectly well who the Prime Minister was.

Her visitor had introduced himself only as 'The Professor', his anonymity being, he said, essential both to his own security and to the success of his mission. She had never known him as anything else. Furthermore, when questioned by Captain Cholmondeley about his appearance, she realised that on each of the few occasions on which they'd met, he had somehow contrived always to keep his face in shadow. She did not know what he looked like. The day after this first meeting, Bessie, at his invitation had gone to an address in Carlton House Terrace, the Headquarters of the British Secret Service. Here, she had been shown straight into the office of the Commander himself.

'The Professor, no doubt?' suggested Sherlock

'Well, 'course,' said Bessie, surprised at the obviousness of the question.

Here, the Professor had told her that he had been visiting the theatre regularly for a week or more, each time just to catch her performance as Queen Victoria in the patriotic monologue 'The Widow of Windsor.'

'He said as 'ed never seen no one more like the Queen than I was, and as it were in my power to save 'er Majesty's life, like, *if* I'd be so good . . .'

'To save her life?' said Captain Cholmondeley, incredulously.

'That's what 'e said, duckie,' said Bessie sharply.

She then went on to describe how the Professor had appealed to her patriotism and her sense of duty; how she'd been promised a State pension of fifty pounds a year for life; how she had finally been persuaded to undertake the task; how very few members of the Royal Household were, of necessity, privy to the plan; how she had then been introduced to Colonel Turnbull, Jasper and Ranjeet; how they had devised the 'cover' of 'Mrs Turnbull'; how she'd been moved to Pendargh Manor to undergo the necessary training; how the Queen was to be drugged at Lancaster and 'switched' at Preston; and how she, Bessie Bright, was finally to end up installed at Windsor.

'Two days after I gets to Windsor,' she continued, 'I was to receive this Indian Prince, d'you see . . .'

'Dhuleep Singh!' exclaimed Sherlock.

''Ow d'you know?' said Bessie, flabberghasted.

'Call it an inspired guess,' said Sherlock. 'And I'll tell you something else I know. The object of your operation was to secure the Eye of the Peacock.'

'Peacock?' said Bessie, not quite sure what he was talking about. She'd heard nothing about no peacocks.

Sherlock glanced across at Captain Cholmondeley who nodded an assent for Sherlock to explain, which he then did with obvious delight.

'You see,' he said, 'Dhuleep Singh was the twelve-year-old ruler of the Punjab when, some twenty years ago, it was annexed by Britain. He was then 'persuaded' to present as a gift to the Queen, India's most precious possession – the Koh-i-Noor Diamond – that exquisite, priceless jewel that had once formed the eye of the peacock in the ancient Peacock Throne of Delhi. A jewel which had passed into his safe-keeping from his father, and a stone of epic significance to the Sikhs.'

124

'I see!' said John Whitney. 'And you think he'd now like to see it returned to India?'

'I dare say he'd like to,' said Sherlock. 'He probably thinks the Queen has about as much right to the Koh-i-Noor as *he* has to Windsor Castle. But I doubt he was directly involved in the plot.'

Bessie confirmed that he was not. ''E just wanted to see it again; to hold it again. But when he'd done and given it back, *I* was to swap it for the one faked up by Greasley.'

'Didn't I tell you that man was a glass-cutter! Doctor my foot!' whooped Sherlock.

'You were to *swap* it?' said Cholmondeley.

'I'm a dab at sleight of hand, dearie,' continued Bessie with immense pride. 'My old man could 'ave palmed the Crown Jewels. 'E was "The Amazin' Marvello". Fourteen pigeons up one sleeve – and a parakeet under 'is 'at!'

Captain Cholmondeley's eyes grew wider with each revelation. 'And tell me,' went on the officer, 'how were you and the diamond to be returned from Palace life to the outside world again? And what was then to become of the diamond?'

'Simple,' said Bessie. 'I'd just go for a walk in the park one day. She's always doin' it. Wanders off. One lady-in-waitin'. Make sure its an old 'un, you can leave 'er miles be'ind. Slip off. Get picked up by old Turnbull, who's brought 'er Maj down from Preston in the carriage and propped 'er under a tree. She comes to a bit giddy, don't remember much. They thinks it's just another nasty turn, don't they?'

'But how was this supposed to save Her Majesty's life and who really wanted the diamond? Am I not correct in thinking it was the Professor?' asked Sherlock.

'*I* don't know!' shouted Bessie angrily. 'Go and ask bleedin' Gladstone!'

By now the three men were helplessly unable to suppress their laughter. They roared. Bessie's look of outraged innocence, indicative of the dawning realisation that politics is a dirty business, only made things worse.

And so it all ended. The weeks that followed were among the dullest of Sherlock's entire life, confined as he was to the routine of the little house at Pendargh.

There was, however, to be one more surprise. It came a few days before Christmas when he was called urgently to the doctors' surgery and there informed that he, John and Charlotte Whitney, George Sowerbutts, Captain Cholmondeley, and even Newbugs, had been summoned to Windsor on Thursday 8 February 1872 where the Queen wished to thank them all in person.

So, in the event, Christmas came and went in a haze of high expectation. Then on a cold February morning a strangely assorted party arrived at Windsor Castle. They were graciously received by Her Majesty who had the Koh-i-Noor Diamond brought in specially for them to see. She impressed upon them the need for complete secrecy in the affair, lest anti-Indian feeling be fermented in the country. 'It shall be as if it had never occurred,' she commanded. Her thanks were then warmly expressed and each of them was rewarded in some suitable manner. Captain Cholmondeley was gazetted Major; John Whitney was appointed Physician-in-Ordinary to the Royal Household; old George Sowerbutts was given a chronometer that had once belonged to her uncle 'Sailor Billy'; Newbugs was, after some deliberation and a little prompting from Sherlock, given a post on the Royal Estates at Balmoral; and Sherlock himself received a remarkably fine emerald tie-pin. (It was, incidentally, this same pin that he was wearing when he returned to Windsor in the late November of 1895 to receive Her Majesty's thanks for his part in recovering The Bruce-Partington Plans. Doctor Watson's assumption about the pin was thus quite incorrect, for though it was indeed a gift from 'a certain gracious lady', it was one that had been given under a vow of secrecy some twenty-three years earlier!).

They hired a gig to carry them from Preston Station to Pendargh on the return, and a merrier party can seldom have been seen travelling that road. It was the last time they were all to be together.

One by one now, as spring came, Sherlock's friends departed for new places. Newbugs left for Balmoral – and sent Aunt Rachel into transports of anger by calling at the front rather than the kitchen door to say 'Good-bye'. (Sherlock had to remind him that he was going with the object of becoming a game-keeper and that he would *not* be requiring the snares that dangled from his trousers pockets).

Shortly after this John and Charlotte Whitney left for London. They picnicked the day before in the hide-away in the woods, Sherlock, John and Charlotte, and George Sowerbutts. Sowerbutts had given Sherlock an old hair-trigger pistol and they all sat round and were deafened as he demonstrated his prowess by shooting the letters 'V.R.' in bullet-pocks in the end wall of the hut where Natty Dan had died. 'For Remembrance,' he said moodily. And no one knew quite what to say.

Later, he fetched from his pocket a pipe he'd bought

himself during the Windsor trip. He filled it laboriously with shag tobacco from a brand new leather pouch, and lit it. Soon the hut was full of acrid smoke, everyone's eyes were streaming, and Sherlock, between puffs, was coughing violently.

It was not a very happy afternoon. Next morning John and Charlotte Whitney were gone. Within a week or so of their departure there was a sad farewell to Mrs Cunliffe who was leaving Aunt Rachel's to get married. In view of the imminent departure of this good and faithful servant the little house was, on this last Saturday in April, in a state of some commotion. In the few minutes left before her cab came, Mrs Cunliffe managed to snatch a few moments alone with Sherlock.

'If you was to say, "don't go", I'd not go, you know,' she said.

'Mrs Cunliffe,' said Sherlock. 'I gave your Tom the strictest instructions that he was to stand no more nonsense from you, but was to marry you forthwith.'

'You'll always be welcome at our house in London,' she said. 'You know that, don't you?'

'I do, Mrs Cunliffe. Or "Mrs Hudson" as I suppose I must get used to calling you. And what exactly is your address to be?'

'Two-twenty-one Baker Street, sir,' she said.

'I shall make a point of calling on you there one day.'

'I do hope so, sir,' she said. 'Good-bye!' She threw her arms around him and her eyes filled with tears.

It was, of course, some good few years later, after her second widowing, that these two met again and Sherlock rented from her that half of the Baker Street house that was designated 221*B*.